Stranded with the Psycho

BY

Annabelle Winters

Copyright Notice

Copyright © 2020 by Annabelle Winters
All Rights Reserved by Author
www.annabellewinters.com
ab@annabellewinters.com

If you'd like to copy, reproduce, sell, or distribute any part of this text, please obtain the explicit, written permission of the author first. Note that you should feel free to tell your spouse, lovers, friends, and coworkers how happy this book made you. Have a wonderful evening!

Cover Design by S. Lee

ISBN: 9798688533569

0 1 2 3 4 5 6 7 8 9

BOOKS BY ANNABELLE WINTERS

THE CURVES FOR SHEIKHS SERIES

Curves for the Sheikh
Flames for the Sheikh
Hostage for the Sheikh
Single for the Sheikh
Stockings for the Sheikh
Untouched for the Sheikh
Surrogate for the Sheikh
Stars for the Sheikh
Shelter for the Sheikh
Shared for the Sheikh
Assassin for the Sheikh
Privilege for the Sheikh
Ransomed for the Sheikh
Uncorked for the Sheikh
Haunted for the Sheikh
Grateful for the Sheikh
Mistletoe for the Sheikh
Fake for the Sheikh

THE CURVES FOR SHIFTERS SERIES

Curves for the Dragon
Born for the Bear
Witch for the Wolf
Tamed for the Lion
Taken for the Tiger

THE CURVY FOR HIM SERIES

The Teacher and the Trainer
The Librarian and the Cop
The Lawyer and the Cowboy
The Princess and the Pirate

The CEO and the Soldier
The Astronaut and the Alien
The Botanist and the Biker
The Psychic and the Senator

The CURVY FOR THE HOLIDAYS Series
Taken on Thanksgiving
Captive for Christmas
Night Before New Year's
Vampire's Curvy Valentine
Flagged on the Fourth
Home for Halloween

The CURVY FOR KEEPS Series
Summoned by the CEO
Given to the Groom
Traded to the Trucker
Punished by the Principal
Wifed by the Warlord

The DRAGON'S CURVY MATE Series
Dragon's Curvy Assistant
Dragon's Curvy Banker
Dragon's Curvy Counselor
Dragon's Curvy Doctor
Dragon's Curvy Engineer
Dragon's Curvy Firefighter
Dragon's Curvy Gambler

The CURVY IN COLLEGE Series
The Jock and the Genius
The Rockstar and the Recluse
The Dropout and the Debutante
The Player and the Princess
The Fratboy and the Feminist

WWW.ANNABELLEWINTERS.

STRANDED WITH THE PSYCHO

BY

ANNABELLE WINTERS

1
<u>SLAY</u>

"That's Slay. He's a psycho."

"Aren't they all?"

"Not like him." Johnson, self-proclaimed Head of the Prison Guards and sadist motherfucker who's killed more inmates than some of the murderers in here, slams his nightstick against the white-painted iron bars of my cage. I don't even open my eyes. My breathing stays so steady my chest barely moves. "Slay's the only one in X Block who gets his own cell on account of his nasty habit of killing his roommates."

My dry lips twist into a smile, and I lick them with my python of a tongue. I don't eat my victims, but the rumors about my methods have me doing all kinds of sick shit. I welcome the rumors—the worse the better. The more they fear me, the more powerful I become.

"Didn't kill that last guy." My eyes stay closed, my voice deep and lazy in a way I know will get Johnson's little curlies all prickly. He's an asshole, and if I were already on Death Row, I'd have broken his neck and worn his scalp like a hat. But for some odd reason they gave me life without the possibility of parole and not the hangman's noose (yeah, I know they don't hang us no more, but I think you can request it instead of the injection). Some say life without parole is worse than a needle in the arm. I disagree. I might be psychotic, but I ain't got a death wish. I was never one of those killers who secretly wanted to get caught and be put out of his self-loathing misery. I was never miserable. I liked to kill. It's what I was born to do. My fate. My destiny. And it's never wrong to follow your destiny.

"That's right," says Johnson. "Last guy hung himself with his sheets while you watched."

"Better than TV." I smile again, moving my head against the gray cinderblock wall as I shift on the steel bench that's bolted into the rough concrete floor which is stained with black streaks of old blood. "Hey, when you gotta go, you gotta go."

Johnson slams that nightstick against the bars again, trailing it along the metal and sneering. He's showing off for the new guard who's getting the grand tour, and I silently clench my fists and tighten my powerful haunches. "You're a sick sonofabitch, Slay. Looking forward to watching you die in here." That nightstick bumps across the bars again as Johnson paces like a zookeeper taunting a caged lion. That usually doesn't end well for the zookeeper if the lion gets out of his cage. It's not going to end well for Johnson.

And now I flick my eyes open and in one swift motion leap off my metal seat, reaching out and grabbing the end of the nightstick and *yanking* it towards me so hard Johnson gets rammed face-first into the iron bars. With a grin I reach my fingers through and shove them up his nostrils, tearing them wide open as Johnson screams like a cheerleader in overtime. The freckle-faced rookie gapes like a goldfish, and I bark at him like a wolf, the shock sending him over the edge. The rookie's eyes show their whites, his head tilts to the left, and he crumples to the floor like a pancake getting folded over. Then I reach my other hand through the bars, grab Johnson's throat, and squeeze slow and steady, my green eyes shining brighter as Johnson's gray pupils go dull and finally fade to zero like I've seen a dozen times before. Well, maybe more than a dozen. I ain't a math guy.

My minds snaps into focus as Johnson drops like a sack of soybeans. I already know the cameras are rolling, and the only reason the alarm hasn't been sounded is because the guard is probably in the bathroom jerking off to an image of his mom. One glance at the passed-out rookie, another at the keys and handgun on Johnson's belt, and the plan unfolds even though I hadn't planned shit.

Vision narrows as I slide the big key into the hole and turn. The clink is heavy and satisfying, and I grin as I take Johnson's gun. Then I raise an eyebrow, rub my jaw, and grab Johnson's walkie too.

Two slaps on the rookie's face and he's awake and gasping. I grab him by the hair and get him to his feet, pushing him forward as I chamber a bullet in the Glock just as the alarm wails and the red-and-white strobes go nuts. I'm the only one in the isolation wing, but already I hear the other inmates hollering and cheering even though they have no idea what's going on. I consider tossing them the keys, but I need them to get out. Besides, all those guys are killers, and letting them out means we're all dead. The guards would open their arsenal and mow us down like my grandpa used to do with crabgrass after drinking Jack Daniels all night.

"I got a hostage and I'm coming out," I say into the walkie before tossing it over my shoulder and jamming the Glock between the whimpering rookie's shoulder blades.

I let myself out of X Block, smiling when I step into the circular atrium with entrances to all the other cell blocks. There's ten stories of cells rising up all around me, and it's raining toilet paper and hailing toothbrushes and pennies and cigarette butts as the inmates toss whatever they can fit through the bars like it's a parade. Every guard's got his gun aimed at me, but I've got my back to the wall and a rookie as a human shield. So long as no one gets behind me, I can pull this off.

"Hold your fire," says the Warden. He looks at me and sighs, stroking his silver goatee and then running his hand through his thinning gray hair. "Listen, Slay. This is dumb, even for you. The moment you break out, there'll be a shoot-on-sight order on your ass. Surrender now and . . ."

He trails off, and I know he saw that Johnson's dead. That means I just got upgraded from life-without-parole to the death penalty. It also means I got nothing to lose now. My odds are better out there than in here.

So I spit on the floor and gesture to the big main door that won't open with Johnson's keys. The Warden hesitates, but then he glances over at the guys in the bulletproof booth and they hit the button. The door grinds and squeals like this is an ancient vault, and I move quick with my hostage, keeping my back to the wall, my gun flush with the rookie's skull.

Now we're in the prison yard, and I blink in the sunshine. Coulda sworn it was the middle of the night. Guess being locked up in a windowless cell with my sun-privileges taken away messes up the body-clock. I watch as the rusty metal gates finally swing open, and a moment later I'm looking out at the open desert of Arizona, nothing but scrubland and rattlesnakes this far in the boonies. One good thing about being so far from a town is that it'll take hours for Federal Marshalls to get out here to pursue my psycho ass.

I squint at the sun. Then I look down at the rookie's wrist, grunt, and rip off his watch. Mid afternoon, which means that way is south to the Mexican border. Probably fifty miles, maybe more. No way I can make it without water. I consider asking the Warden for a vehicle and a head start in exchange for the hostage, but taking a prison truck will only make it easier to find me. I know how to survive in the desert. I'll find water. And if I don't? Well, I'll drink this fucker's blood.

"Just kidding. Drinking your blood will only make me more thirsty," I say with a grim wink before realizing he can't read my thoughts. For me thoughts and speech are the same thing now—when you're in solitary, your thoughts get so loud you hear them, and your voice sounds so strange it's like a dream. Soon you lose track of the line between thinking and talking, reality and fantasy, maybe even life and death.

Hell, even this whole escape thing feels like fantasy, don't it? I never planned for this to happen today, but suddenly I'm out here in the sunshine, the open desert stretched before me like an ocean, nothing but waves of sand and distant horizon in my way. Fuck, this feels like fate, don't it?

Maybe it is fate, I think as I back away from the prison gates and into the boundless desert. It's got that feel to it, don't it? Just like I knew it was fate when I killed that sonofabitch who hurt my sister. Killed him with my big young hands, looking into his eyes without flinching. No guilt in my heart when I watched those eyes go wide with fear and then switch off like the lights just went out.

Goodbye Grandpa, I'd whispered to the old pervert. I'll see you in hell.

2
__SIENNA__

"This must be what hell feels like."

"I've heard hell is cold," I say, glancing over at Carl as he mops his brow with a green-and-red bandana that I think he bought specifically for this trip. "I'd much rather be in a hot desert than a cold one."

"Fuck that." Carl rubs his mouth with his sleeve and reaches for the water between the seats. He drains the plastic bottle and tosses it into the backseat. "Hand me another."

I glance down at the plastic-wrapped case of bottled water and do a quick count. There's another case in the back, but we're miles from the nearest gas station—and more miles from the nearest town. "Later," I say.

Carl whips his head toward me, his blue eyes cold in the desert sun. "Excuse me? Hand me a fucking bottle, Sienna! Now!"

I flinch at the tone, frowning and slowly reaching between my bare brown legs to wrestle a bottle from the pack. I take my time handing it to Carl, swallowing my anger as my heat rises—and not in the good way. In fact the *good* kind of heat hasn't risen in months with Carl, and any hopes I'd had of this trip rekindling that fire are being steadily choked out by his attitude. Though I guess you can't *re*kindle a fire that never burned too bright in the first place.

"Two more hours to the site." I glance at my watch and then lean forward to check the sun's position. "How about we not fight until we get there?"

Carl tightens his thin lips and sighs. He turns the temperature-control knob toward the blue side. It doesn't turn because it's already on the coldest setting.

"Actually we should turn off the air-conditioning for a bit. The engine might overheat," I say, glancing at Carl's nails, which are rough and short from his constant nibbling.

"How the hell can air-conditioning heat up the engine? Air-conditioning is cold."

I raise an eyebrow and consider checking Carl's temperature to see if he's got heatstroke. Nope. Carl just doesn't know shit about cars. That's OK. I know enough for both of us. Dad taught me a couple of things before he left this earth to become starlight.

I let go of the topic, reaching for the dashboard radio and scanning through the stations. We're so far from a town that I'm more likely to pick up a distress signal from outer space than a Top 40 station, and finally I sigh and pull out my phone to find some music.

"Huh. No signal on my iPhone. Not even roaming." I hold the phone up to the window. Still nothing. "I guess we're listening to the same ten songs I've got saved on my phone."

"What the fuck is that?"

I glance up, ready to get into it with Carl for his rudeness. But I see he's squinting up ahead to his left, and I blink and then gasp when I see a man the size of a tractor standing by the dusty desert road. He's shirtless under the sun, his body bronzed and glistening, with ripples of contoured muscle that makes me press my legs together at the thigh as a weird tingle snakes its way under my panties. The man turns as we approach, and even from this distance his eyes shine green like emeralds, his thick hair black and long, a heavy mustache on his angular face that's scarred and sunburned in the most entrancing way. At first I wonder if he's a desert mirage, but then he pops up his thumb that's thicker than a hoagie bun.

"Stop," I say softly as Carl tenses up and then presses down on the gas, revving the engine and spinning the back tires on the sand-covered road.

"We're not stopping," Carl says through his teeth, wiping his mouth on his silk sleeve, his knuckles white on the wheel. "Are you crazy? Look at that guy!"

"Just stop, Carl. It's the right thing to do out here in the desert. He could die if we don't give him a ride."

"Better him than me," says Carl, swallowing hard and licking his lips as we get close. Then, just as we pass the scarred monster of the desert, Carl turns his head, grins, and flips off the guy, who's got his thumb up to his lips now, those green eyes locked in on me like I'm the only person in the car, maybe in the world.

"He wants water, not a ride!" I reach for a bottle to toss out the window since Carl is too scared to stop. But Carl has the power windows locked down, and so I snap off my seatbelt and pop the sunroof.

Somehow I maneuver my big boobs up through the hole, and then I yelp when I realize the left strap of my tanktop just got caught on the edge and my boob just popped out like a pointy-nosed porpoise!

I hurl the bottle at the guy and frantically cover my boob, but I already feel the shirtless beast's eyes on me, his hungry gaze taking in every detail of my dark nipple, the swell of my bosom. Once I'm covered I meet his gaze, and I see him smile as we leave him in our dust. Again I get that tingle between my thighs, and I let my gaze travel down his bare torso, take in the heaviness of his chest, the deep, dark V of his tight abdomen, the deadly cut of his powerful haunches, the massive bulge at the crotch of gray pants with a navy stripe along each side like they're part of a uniform. They're also way too small for him. The pants barely get down past his calves, and the button isn't even in the neighborhood of being able to close. The only reason they're staying up is because they're so darned tight.

I stare into those green eyes as the man fades into the distance, and I sigh and wave and then shrug my shoulders like I can't do anything about it. He breaks into a grin, his dark face lighting up, his green eyes shining in a vaguely crazy way as he blows me a kiss that makes me wonder if he's already in heatstroke territory. Suddenly I decide that we need to stop, that we can't leave him stranded in the desert, a hundred miles from everything. That's as good as us killing him ourselves, and I don't kill people.

So I gesture to the guy to hold on, and then I prepare to duck back into the car and do what it takes to get Carl to pull over. But just as I get my head down past the roof, the car makes an awful choking sound, and then with a sputtering sigh the engine dies!

Carl is cursing like a scared sailor as the car rolls to a dusty stop, and I plop back into my seat and glance at the blinking lights on the dashboard.

"Overheated." I turn off the air-conditioning and kill the power so the battery doesn't drain. I want to say I told him so, but I just think it instead. As rude as Carl is to me, I was raised to be polite even to my worst enemy. "Give it a few minutes and then we'll try again."

Carl glances into the rearview mirrors, and I almost chuckle when I see him surreptitiously hit the power lock about five times. "Hand me my knife," he says, barely getting the words out.

This time I do laugh. "You mean the Swiss Army knife? Relax, Carl. I'm sure he isn't pissed that you flipped him off and left him to die."

Carl holds on to the steering wheel like his pasty fingers are stuck to the plastic. "He doesn't look happy. Oh, fuck, Sienna. I'm gonna die out here. I knew it. I had a bad feeling about this trip. I knew I shouldn't have come. Should've just ended it before the trip instead of waiting till we got back. But I'd have lost the deposit on the rental car."

"Wait, *what*?" I'm watching the guy amble towards us like he's got all the time in the world, swigging that water I tossed to him. He pours some over his head, and then he slides the half-empty bottle into a cargo pocket on his undersized gray pants. Only now does Carl's babbling register, and I focus on his wishy-washy blue eyes that are darting all over the place like discolored pinballs. I stare dumbfounded as Carl melts down like a stick of butter in the sun, and I'm so disgusted I don't even bother to acknowledge that he just admitted he was going to dump me after this trip.

Carl bites his lip and his breathing quickens. Mine does too, and I don't know if it's because I'm hurt and angry or if it's because that bare-chested mass of walking muscle is bearing down on us. I glance back through the seats, gasping when I see the broad looming shadow move close like a giant bird of prey swooping down on us.

"Ohgod, ohgod, ohgod, he's got a gun," Carl

shrieks, clicking the locks again as I peer back and see the shining black handgun dangling from the man's left hand.

I gulp and glance down at my black tank-top, my smooth brown cleavage looking heavier than I remember. A chill goes through me when I remember inadvertently flashing that guy, and I wonder if I'm gonna have to barter my boobs to save my sniveling boyfriend's life—not to mention my own, I guess.

I watch as the man strolls past the car. He's so tall I can't even see his face, just his bronzed midsection that's cut like an Aztec warrior. He stops by the drivers side window and taps on the glass with his gun barrel. I glance at Carl and groan when I see that my protector's got his eyes closed and is still gripping that steering wheel like a baby clutching the safety bars of his crib. Clearly Carl will not be making his stand with a Swiss Army knife in hand, and so I lean across and unlock the doors and hit the window button.

"Hi," I say to the guy as the window squeaks down. The man's scent flows in with the dry desert air, and when I inhale his smoky musk that tingle goes through me again, making my pubic hairs prick up like something just touched my pussy. "We overheated," I say lamely.

The man slowly leans his big body down and

peers into the car. His gaze lands on my lips first, and I lick them like I can't help it. Then he looks into my eyes, holding the gaze long enough to make me sweat. Now a fleeting but shameless glance at my boobs that feel dangerously vulnerable in a tank-top, and finally the man blinks and then frowns at Carl.

"What's with him?" the man grunts. Carl is sitting absolutely still, eyes closed tight, barely breathing like he thinks if he stays quiet no one will see him.

"He's scared." I blink when he looks at me again. "I am too."

The man squares his scarred jaw, his mustache twitching as he trains those green eyes on me. "No, you're not. You got more balls than your boyfriend does." He pokes Carl in the cheek with the black barrel of the gun. Carl wriggles like a worm and lets out a yelp. But he keeps those eyes closed, and I'm almost impressed by how well he can deny reality. "Yo. Lemme see that finger, bud."

I frown, and then my throat tightens when the man reaches into the car and grabs Carl's wrist. I'm not sure what's going on, but before I can say or do a thing, the man grabs Carl's middle finger, twists it like a Twizzler, and then yanks it back until it snaps like a twig on the forest floor!

Carl's eyes pop open like a possessed corpse coming to life. His mouth goes wide in a silent scream, and I cover my face and hyperventilate about four hundred times in the next three seconds. Now the fear hits, but I don't handle fear by freezing up. I deal with fear head-on. I fight.

And so I lean down and slide my hand into the front pocket of my backpack, feeling around for that Swiss Army knife. I palm it and draw my hand back as Carl finally finds his voice and screams like a band of banshees. Two deep breaths as I spread my thighs and drop my hands between my legs so I can open the knife without him seeing. I feel the cold steel of the blade, and before I lose my shit I lunge across the seat and go for the man's gunhand, slashing wildly in the hopes he drops the gun into the car so I can grab it!

I manage to cut him, but clearly he's been cut before and it's about as meaningful as being bitten by a gnat. He barely flinches as blood rushes from the cuts, and as dread rolls through me like the tide coming in, he reaches past Carl and grabs my throat with a hand bigger than the moonroof.

My eyes bulge as I slash at his wrist, but it's like chipping away at a stone pillar with a toothpick. A moment later he's pulled me across Carl's lap, and I gurgle and tremble when he brings his head so close I can see every line on his face, read his violent history like a map, see the dark truth in his green eyes:

The truth that this man has killed before . . .

And that he's going to kill again.

Now a strange peace ripples through that rising tide of dread, and I shudder out a breath as I prepare to meet my dead parents in the Great Beyond. My gaze is fixed on those green eyes, and I see the coldness in there, sense the desolation behind that focus, feel the loneliness that must come with the territory when you're a killer.

I breathe again, only now realizing that although he's gripping tight, he isn't squeezing. I'm not being choked—not yet, at least. He's just staring into my eyes like he sees something. Something that surprises him. Something that startles him. Something that shocks him.

And something that might save me.

He blinks, and when his eyelids reveal those green orbs again I'm startled to see I might be right. There's a flicker of warmth in there. A hint of humanity. A sliver of salvation. He moves his thumb on my neck, stroking my skin as he leans close and sniffs me like a monster deciding if I'm good enough to eat. Or kill.

"I should kill you," he whispers, sniffing me all the way to my ear, his hot breath sending wisps of my dark hair spinning like dervishes doing their dance. "But I want to keep you instead. So I think I'll do that. I'll keep you."

I stare as the words flow around me like clouds. His rough thumb strokes my throat again, and I swear I feel my pussy tighten and release its wetness into my blue cotton panties that have ridden deep up the sides of my thick thighs and into my big ass. Finally his words make it through to my brain, and as if in a dream I understand that a switch just got flipped in this monster. He was going to kill me, but something made him stop.

Something made him decide to keep me instead.

And as I stare into his empty green eyes that are searching my face with a yearning that I can feel in my throat, the man inhales my scent a third time and slowly pulls back.

Then, still holding my throat, those green eyes locked, he leans in and kisses me.

He kisses me hard and full, right on the mouth, crushing my lips against my teeth, jamming his salty tongue into my mouth even as I try to clamp shut.

He kisses me.

By God, he kisses me.

3
<u>SLAY</u>

Her lips taste like caramelized sugar, the kind my sister used to make on an open flame. I move my fingers up and down her smooth neck, kissing her hard again and then letting go and pushing her back to her side of the car. My body yearns to savage her right now, but that'll have to wait. Better to wait. I need to wait.

Wait until I can let this strange energy work its way through my body and mind. An energy that gripped my heart when I looked into this beauty's brown eyes, touched her soft skin, tasted her caramel lips. I've been locked up for eight years, but this ain't just about feeling a warm pussy around my thick cock again. It's about more than that, and I shake my head three times like a dog at the beach, trying to clear away the thought I'd gotten earlier when escape presented itself to me like a gift from fate.

Was I meant to run into this woman on a dusty desert road, I wonder as I cast a glance in her direction. She's sitting bolt upright, eyes wide and staring straight ahead, chest moving so fast her boobs shake and shimmy. I see the outline of her nipples, and from that peek I got earlier I know those nubs are big like dinner plates, dark like rainclouds. I want to pinch them raw, suck them tender, slap my heavy cock against them before I titty-fuck her roughly on my way to her mouth. Hell, I should kill this sad excuse for a man and fuck his woman outside on the hood. Tear her clothes to shreds. Eat her soaked panties just to get a taste of her cunt. Grab her by the ankles and hold her legs up high, let the sun blaze down on our bronzed bodies as I pump her so full she overflows onto the hot metal.

"What are you going to do to me?" comes a whisper through my vision. I growl at being brought back to reality. I'm so used to isolation in a windowless cell that my imagination is more vivid than a Dali painting. It's the sniveling guy talking. He just saw me claim his woman and all he's worried about is himself.

"Kill you and eat you." I lean on the window, my face so close to his I bet he can smell his woman's essence on my tongue. She's still in stunned silence, and I focus on this idiot, grinning when he starts to sob. "Relax," I say, thumping his shoulder so hard his teeth rattle. "I don't eat people. I'm not that kind of psycho."

"But you *are* going to kill me, aren't you?" The guy finally looks into my eyes, and I stare dead into his blue holes that barely have any life-force in them. In a way this guy died years before he ever crossed my path. That's what happens to a man who chases safety and security instead of giving himself the freedom to chase his desires, take what he wants without making excuses. That's what a man is. We've descended from the cavemen who survived, men who killed anyone who looked at them funny, men who fucked every cavewoman in sight—regardless of whether she had another man or not.

I sigh and pull open the drivers side door. "Get out." I step back as the guy steps out and immediately crumples to the dirt because his legs are about as sturdy as rubberbands. I sigh again and scratch my jaw with the barrel of the gun. I already let that rookie guard go after taking his clothes. Will I have to let another coward live? Probably. I only kill when I get that vibe. This would be like killing a man when he's down, and I ain't that guy. Still, I can scare some balls into this guy. Maybe it even helps him man up in the future. Too late to save his girl, but maybe he grows from the experience.

I exhale hard and then glance over at the woman, who's finally caught her breath and is rubbing her throat. "What's your name?" I ask.

She frowns and looks around. Then she gasps when she sees Carl on the ground outside the open door. "Don't kill him."

"Why not?" I say, leaning on the open door, my weight making the car lean my way.

She thinks. "He doesn't deserve to die."

I chuckle. "Not how it works, Sugar."

"My name's not Sugar."

I shrug. "I asked. You didn't answer. I don't ask twice. So now your name is Sugar."

She blinks and swallows, pulling on her tank-top so I can't see down to the valley between her rises. "Sienna," she says hesitantly. Then she glances at her boyfriend and back into my eyes, her gaze firm now, her strength of will surprising me.

Most people crumble like this guy when face to face with the grim reaper that works through me. Not her, though. Strange that she picked this guy for a boyfriend.

Won't matter soon, I remind myself as I tuck the gun down the back of my pants and crack my knuckles. I can handle a gun as well as I can handle my cock, but there's no need to attract attention. I doubt the US Marshalls picked up my trail after I used the old Apache tricks for covering my tracks, but I can't be too careful. The Mexican border's not far, but a lot can happen between here and there.

"Any last words?" I grab the punk by the hair. He screams as I pull him to his feet. "That's not a word, but whatever floats your boat, buddy." My hand snaps around his throat like it has for dozens of men . . . all of whom will be waiting for me in hell when I get there.

"You stop that!" comes Sienna's voice. I glance into the car and realize she's gone, and I whip my head to the left just in time to see her holding that bloody pocket-knife with both hands like she's wielding Excalibur.

I relax my grip on her man and turn, still holding the guy by the hair like a rag-doll. I glance down at him and then up at her. "You going to fight me to save his ass? You know I could kill you both with one hand chopped off."

"Great," she says, slashing the air with that tiny knife. "So let me chop it off. Let's see if you can walk the talk, you big pussy."

Now I let go of the guy. He drops to the dirt and scrambles away behind the vehicle. I stretch my thick arms out wide, lean left and right to crack my back, twist my neck to loosen up the sinews. I square my jaw and then bite my lip, my throat tightening when I taste her sugar still sweet in my mouth. I know I'm not going to hurt her. Yeah, I could overpower her in a flash, bring her to her knees so fast she'd leave her hair behind. But I'm not worried about that puny knife or getting cut again. The only thing on my mind is that girl holding the knife. I saw something in those eyes earlier. Tasted something on those lips.

Something that puzzles me.

Something that scares me.

Something that tells me if I hurt either of them I also kill any chance I have with her.

The thought makes me hesitate, and I lick my lips and shake my head as my hands go to my hips. Why the fuck do I care about my "chances" with this girl? She's mine and that's all there is to it. The question isn't *if* I'm gonna get what I want. It's *when*.

"You leave him alone," she says again, shifting her hips, parting those brown thighs as she plants her feet wide to get leverage. She's scared, but she's standing her ground. That's real courage. This girl is something. She's someone. Someone who could ride shotgun with me. Just gotta make sure I break her in right.

But the first thing I gotta show her is that she needs to upgrade from Mister Pussycat here. It ain't a good sign that she thinks this dipshit is in her league. Maybe her parents did a number on her, making her lose faith in herself. Maybe it was some other guy in her past. Don't matter. She's mine now, and she needs to believe that she's up to the task.

So I hold my big hands out, waist high, fingers spread. Lazy grin on my burned lips. "All right, Killer Queen. I'll leave your boyfriend alone. For now, at least." I take a slow breath when I see her blink and glance at the coward. "But seriously. You really would have fought me to save his ass?"

"Still might," she snarls. Doesn't pull it off, though. It's a little snarl, like wolves at play.

I run my gaze down along those thick thighs that glisten like smooth young tree-trunks in the yellow sun. I want my face in there, up between those legs, her pussy pouring down on me as I lap up her juice like a thirsty dog. She shifts her feet, and when I glance into her eyes I see that she felt something between her legs, right where my mind was. Her mind went there too, and I'll bet those panties are warm and damp right now, wetter than this fuckhead ever got her.

I turn to fuckhead pussycake. "Yo, studman. Come on out. Reaper ain't coming for you yet." I wait, but the guy's still hiding behind the truck like an ostrich. I clap my hands once, sending brown dust into the air as I stroll around the front of the car. The clown decides just then to make a run for it, take his chances in the open desert and leave his woman for the big bad wolf. "I guess it's every man for himself, Sugar," I grunt as the idiot stumbles over a tiny sandhill and howls as he eats the dirt. I glance into their truck, reaching in and grabbing a still-sealed bottle of water. It's nice and heavy. I square my shoulders, plant my feet, and wait for the fool to stand. When he does I draw my arm back and whip the water-bottle, making sure I follow through just like I used to when I whipped those fastballs down the plate so hard nobody in high-school wanted to play catcher. The bottle clocks him at the back of the head just as he stands, and although the plastic's got enough give that it won't crack his skull, it's enough to drop him back to the dirt.

Sienna's watching, and though she gasps and covers her mouth when the bottle hits home, she doesn't say anything. She knows the bottle won't do any real damage. She also knows this guy cares about his own ass and nothing else. Yeah, she sees it—but just in case, let me show her again.

So I reach for my gun and grab Sienna by the arm. I pull her into my body so hard she grabs onto me in shock, her fingers clawing at my muscled abdomen. "Relax," I whisper, holding her in front of me, her soft ass pressing against my monstrous erection. Her scent rises like a serpent, and I inhale deep, my throat rumbling as I smell the musk from her underarms, the warmth from between her thighs, the pungent tang of her pussy. Isolation heightens a man's senses, and Sienna's body is getting every fucking sense high like a kite on cocaine.

"Yo, Speedy Gonzales!" I shout, flicking the safety on and holding the gun to Sienna's temple. The guy's on his feet again, on the move again, slow and lopsided. "Enough of this shit. Come back or I put one in your girl. Maybe two." The guy doesn't turn, and I feel Sienna stiffen. She isn't afraid. She's pissed off. So I grin and double-down. "Then maybe I fuck her dead body and eat her cheeks!"

Sienna whips her head around, her brown eyes wide like a doe on a dewy morning. I wink and lean close, my whisper making her lashes move. "Chill, woman. I'm not that kind of psycho. Don't fuck the dead is one of my rules."

"Nice to know," she says. "But you're still a psycho. What about eating my face?" she demands, sucking in those round cheeks and then blowing out warm air that tickles my lips.

"Vegetarian for twenty years." I wink again and sigh when the guy finally stops and turns. I wave to him and hold the gun to Sienna's head again. Slowly I bring my other hand up to her neck, gently closing my fingers around her smooth skin. She gasps and shudders, and I grind my cock against her nice big ass, pulling her into me as arousal raw and red burns through me.

"If I come back there we're both dead." The guy shrugs and holds his arms out. "Sorry, Sienna. But it wasn't working anyway. I was going to break up before the trip, but—"

"Right. You didn't want to lose the deposit on the rental." Sienna chuckles coldly and glances up at me. "Give me the gun. I'll shoot him myself."

The guy shrieks and restarts his slow escape, and I snort and shove the gun back into my waistband. "No gunshots. Too loud." Then I grunt and nod at Sienna. "I like the sentiment, though. You killed someone before?"

She turns, her pretty face twisted like the wind just changed and it got stuck while she was holding back a sneeze. "Have I *killed* someone? Really? You ask that to everyone you meet?"

I shrug. "Don't meet a lot of people." Then I grin. "And the ones I do meet don't tend to live too long."

Sienna cocks her head, and then she shakes it. "You really are a psycho," she whispers. Then she squints at her fleeing protector, who isn't even very good at protecting his own ass. "He's going to die out there without water or shade or any clue where he's going."

"Yup." I glance at their truck, not concerned about that fool in the least. "Come on. Engine should've cooled down by now. I'll check the water levels and then we can go."

"Go where?"

"Mexico. There's an outlaw town just past the border."

"What's an outlaw town?"

"Take a wild guess, Sugar." I pop the hood and

peer inside. The puny engine belongs on a dirtbike, not an SUV. What the fuck happened to American manufacturing while I was locked up?

"My name's Sienna. Also, I'm not an outlaw, so why would I go to an outlaw town?"

I slam the hood down hard enough to make her jump. "Because you're mine, Sugar. Said I was keeping you. What part of that do you not understand?"

She blinks and crosses her arms under her boobs. "Um, *all* parts of that. Don't understand *any* of it, Psycho."

"No need for name-calling, Sugar," I drawl, taking a step towards her and stopping before I can't stop. "I'm Slay."

"*Slay?*" Her eyebrows go up. Then she rolls those brown eyes at me. "All right. Whatever. Sure." She turns back to the lumbering figure of her deadman-walking boyfriend. "Now can we go get Carl, please? As much as I'd like to let him burn out there, I can't do that. After all, I'm the one who planned this trip."

I take a breath, look around, and then sigh as Sienna turns and starts to walk after Carl. Two long strides and I catch up and walk alongside. "Why the hell are you two city kids way out here, so far from the main highways?"

Sienna points up at the cloudless blue sky. "I'm an astrologer."

I glance up and then rub the back of my head. "Well, that clears it up, Sugar."

She snickers, shooting a sideways glance at me, her dark red lips curling at the corners, my cock moving like it can see her through its hungry cyclops eye. "There's a once-in-a-lifetime star alignment that's going to be visible tonight. The night sky is clearest over a desert, and I mapped out the ideal coordinates." She glances at the sun and then points Southeast. "Couple of hours thataway." Then she sighs as Carl glances over his shoulder and picks up the pace, forcing us to walk faster. "Sucks that I'm going to miss it."

I glance towards the Southeast and then back at Sienna. She's moved ahead of me, and I stare shamelessly at her big buttocks bouncing in perfect time with the thunder of those silky thighs, the swing of those wide hips. She's more woman than I've ever seen, and I know she's going to be able to handle every inch of me, again and again, deeper than any man's ever reached, harder than any man's ever dared.

That sorry excuse for a man is pissing me off,

and I'm about to race ahead and bring him down so we can end this slowpoke chase scene. But just then I hear the throaty roar of a V8 engine, and I whip around, gun drawn, mind spinning as I wonder how the US Marshalls found me so quick.

But one look tells me it's not the law.

Quite the opposite.

It's a dirt-streaked black open-topped Wrangler, fully loaded with two colorful banditos in the front and three more in the bench seats out back. I see the tops of assault rifles, and I catch the glint of mirrored aviator sunglasses and flashes of gold from the grills in their teeth.

"Stay close to me," I snap, my eyes locked on the banditos as they bump and hop their Jeep across the rough open ground, heading right for us. They must have seen the car and then caught sight of the three of us. "Don't say a word."

Sienna moves close to me, and when I pick up her feminine scent again I'm overwhelmed with a desperate need to protect her, to keep her safe, to just fucking *keep* her.

The Wrangler rumbles to a stop in a cloud of dust, and the three banditos in the back tumble out, rifles ready, teeth gleaming like goldmines.

They're all wearing black bandanas with red and yellow stripes and a logo with three intertwined rattlesnakes. I know that logo, and when they approach I drop my gun to the dirt and twist my arm so they can see the prison-tattoo on my left tricep.

Bandito Number One takes off his sunglasses, looks at the tat, and then shifts his teeth-grill with his tongue. He turns to his buddies and mutters something in Spanish. The other two check out my tattoo, and then they all nod at each other and take a step back.

The driver stays in the Jeep, and the last guy hops out of the front seat and runs down Carl with ease, dragging him back to us and shoving him face-first into the gravelly sand. Then all four of the banditos look at Sienna, and I already know what they want.

"This one's mine." I slide my arm around Sienna's waist, surprised when she moves close to me with a willingness that isn't an act. She senses that I'm serious as death about protecting her. She knows I'm her best chance to survive out here.

Bandito Number One slides his mirrored aviators back on his sweat-greased nose. He rubs his scraggly black goatee, grimacing and then scratching his dry, sunburned neck. One good thing about being a mixed-breed mongrel is that I got along with all the different prison gangs, somehow managing to keep myself out of any inter-gang wars. Result is I got my body marked with all their signs, and that's what these banditos just read from my ink. They won't touch me. And hopefully they won't try to touch Sienna.

Number One takes a long look at Sienna. Then he glances at me, touching his glasses as I flex my left pectoral and clench my right fist. I'm outgunned and outnumbered, but this guy's been in enough close-range fights to know that rifles aren't easy to use when you're three feet from your opponent. Chances are I'd break this guy's neck before a single bullet breaks my scarred skin.

The silent standoff continues, and I place my hand against the small of Sienna's back. She's trembling like a mare at the gates, and I keep my big hand flat and steady on her body until she presses herself into my strength and her breathing slows.

And then I see the bandito's Adam's apple move as he swallows, and he grins and nods, moving his attention to Carl, who's on his knees like he's ready to be executed.

"You rich, Gringo?" he says to Carl.

Carl looks up wide-eyed. "Er . . . a little."

"Yeah, he's rich," I say confidently, putting the

pieces together. They have no use for Carl unless they can ransom him, get a payoff in return for letting him go. Not that they'll actually let him go in the end, but at least it'll give him a few more days to enjoy his sad life before they put him out of his misery. Hell, maybe he even makes it out alive if he can negotiate a safe way to get released while still paying them off. "And he sure as hell don't want to die. Good catch, if you ask me."

The bandito nods, snapping his fingers and pointing. Two of his buddies step forward, grabbing Carl by the armpits and dragging him to their Jeep as Sienna's breath catches and she glances wild-eyed up at me. I keep my hand firm against her lower back, reminding her with my eyes that she needs to shut the hell up or no good will come of it. The banditos saddle up and roar away in their Jeep, and Sienna whips around, her face peaked, eyes sharp like daggers.

"We have to save him!" she says.

"He can save himself." I start back towards the truck. Her shadow doesn't move, and I groan and turn. "What? You give a shit about that guy?"

"I give a shit about human life."

"Human life is cheap." I cross my thick arms over my bare chest. "And I just saved yours, so you're welcome. Now come on before those banditos change their mind about you."

Sienna bites her lip, and then she starts walking. "What would they do with me?"

I glance at her, blinking as that sickening feeling of possessiveness grabs me by the throat again. It's a terrifying sensation. Males me think I'd do things for this girl that I'd never do for another living soul. Do things just so I can keep her.

"I tell you and you'd never be able to sleep through the night again," I say as we get to the road and I yank open the drivers side door, pushing the seat all the way back just so I can cram my big body into this toy car.

She gets in and buckles up. "I don't sleep through the night as it is. I'm a stargazer, remember? Gotta be awake at night if you want to see the stars."

"I thought you said planets, not stars," I say as I test the engine and grin when it chugs to life.

She furrows at me. "Surprised you know the difference."

I glare back as I pull onto the road. I turn off the air-conditioning and put down all the windows. The hot air hits me like a slap, but one look at Sienna and I see she loves the heat. I watch as she smiles and closes her eyes to the wind, pulling her hair back and corralling it into a pony-tail that would work great as a hand-hold while I push her mouth down on my cock. "Read a lot in prison," I say, keeping my eyes front and center so I don't give in to the beast in my pants that wants Sienna's ass up in the air, pink slit wide and wet. Still not sure why I'm waiting to claim her—though maybe I just don't want to admit the reason. Don't want to admit that this feels different from every woman I've made mine over the years—everything from whores to housewives, addicts to attorneys, sick bitches with bloodlust worse than mine to giggly college chicks who called me Daddy as I spanked their basketball-shaped bottoms and then took them in the gloryhole. All that was fun, and those memories were good enough to get me through prison. But with Sienna something's different. It's like I don't just want to take her hard, don't just want to ravish her body, don't just want to claim her cunt . . .

I want more than that with her.

I want *all* of her.

Her body, her mind, her heart. Her hopes, her fears, her dreams. I want to comfort her in the night, protect her in the dark, play with her in the sun. I want to see her round and pregnant with my children, her brown breasts heavy with milk, her pretty face shining with the glow of motherhood.

It's fucked up as all hell, but that vision is more vivid than the hallucinations during solitary.

"Will those guys let Carl go if he pays them?" she asks, ignoring my comment about prison in a way that gives me pause. She slides on a pair of gigantic round sunglasses with red plastic frames. The lenses are light and I can still see her eyes. They're smiling at me. She's concerned about Carl, but she's not frozen with fear or trembling with terror. She understands this is serious, that most likely Carl is a dead man either way, that even if she calls the local police they have no hope of tracking those guys before they disappear over the border.

"Maybe they'll let him go," I say softly.

"Sounds like a no." She adjusts her glasses and pulls out a phone from her cargo shorts. I'm about to snatch it and toss it, but I hold back. She turns it on and then waves it about like a wand. "Shit. Still no signal."

"Who you gonna call? Cops? FBI? US Marshalls?"

Sienna turns to me and covers her mouth, her eyes wide behind those light brown lenses. "Oh, right. You probably don't want me to . . . oops. Sorry."

I grunt and stay silent.

She bites her lip and swallows. "So . . . you . . . um . . . kill people?"

I raise an eyebrow and glance at her sideways. "You mean for a living? Nah. It's just a hobby."

She chuckles nervously, pulling at the edges of her cargo shorts. Her toes curl in her sandals, and I smile and focus on the road. "How long have you killed people?" she asks.

I shrug. "Since I was eight, I guess. Yeah, that's it. Eight."

"What happened when you were eight?"

My jaw stiffens and I almost crush the steering wheel as my grip goes tight like a vise. It feels like there's something in my throat, and I swallow hard as I try to fight the warm emotion bubbling up in me. It feels strange, foreign, alien. I'm a cold-blooded killer, aren't I? Why does this girl want to know anything about me? Why is she asking about what happened when I was eight? Why is she asking what nobody's ever asked—no counselor, no friend, no human alive or dead. Nobody.

"I'm listening, Slay," she says, urging me on as I wrestle myself and try to stay on the road. I shoot a glance at her, not sure if this is a trick to get my guard down. She turns her face to me, and just then the sun hits her sideways, the rays glancing off her smooth cheeks, lighting her beauty in a way that makes me feel funny . . . funny like I felt when

Stranded with the Psycho

that chance to escape popped up, sprung me from my cage like it was part of a plan—a plan written in the stars.

Suddenly I realize we're headed Southeast along this road, and I remember what she said about some kind of once-in-a-lifetime planetary alignment. There was a book with horoscopes and shit in the prison library, and I remember a chapter about how the ancient shamans of the old desert used to read the stars and planets to decide the best times for everything from wars to marriages.

And so I take a slow breath, sink back into the seat, and relax my grip on the wheel. Then I turn to her and speak as my mind goes back to that eight-year-old kid, that boy who'd finally grown strong enough to protect his older sister, that boy who learned the secret truth that violence is power. The only form of power.

Or so I thought.

4
SIENNA

I watch Slay like a rabbit watches the hawk circling above. The rabbit isn't sure if the hawk is hunting. She isn't sure if she's the prey. She wonders if she's better off running or standing still.

For now I'm standing still, I decide as Slay glances over at me, those cold green eyes flickering with a light that makes me think there's a human being in there. And didn't I say every human life is precious? Even the life of a remorseless killer? Do I believe that? Can I truly accept that Slay's life is as precious as anyone else's?

"I'm listening, Slay," I say, keeping my gaze on his angular profile that's cut like a canyon ridge.

His skin is dark brown, but the hints of sunburn are fresh, like today's the first he's seen of the sun in weeks, months maybe, perhaps years. "Eight years old, you said." I glance out the window and then back at him. "How many years ago was that? Which month?"

Slay chuckles and tilts his head to the left. I hear his big collarbone click into place. "You gonna do a star-map for my first kill, Sugar?"

"Who was that first kill? Someone close to you?"

He whips his head towards me, those big hands gripping the wheel so tight the stiff plastic bends. Two long, slow breaths, eyes back on the road. I wait, and finally Slay talks.

"I was five when I understood that what Grandpa was doing to Sis was bad," he says slowly, shifting on his seat and clearing his throat. He swallows hard, and I swear I see the child in this monster, a five-year-old boy unsure of himself, unsure of the world. What happens when the first thing you're sure of is a violation so dark it changes you forever?

"How old was your sister?" I say, keeping my voice steady and soft even though my throat feels dry and tight.

"Four years older. I was too small to do anything. Every time I tried, I'd get the belt. Sometimes a fist.

Once a bottle at my head." He grunts. "Picked up the pieces and went for him. Cut him on the leg before he booted me clear across the room." Slay's face hardens. "But I made him bleed, and that showed me I wasn't powerless."

I wince and swallow. "Making someone bleed . . . I guess that's power. Never thought of it that way."

Slay frowns at me. "What is power if not imposing your will on another?"

I touch my neck and glance up at the radiant blue sky, the fireball sun staring down at us like we're the only two people in its light. "Power makes me think of the stars and planets, all of them in their places because of balance. The sun is more powerful than any of the planets, but if it imposed its full power, we'd all be sucked into the sun and burned down to nothing. So real power isn't about imposing yourself on another. It's about finding your place in the universe, helping the heavenly bodies around you be what they were destined to be, shine with a light that reflects your own power."

Slay raises a big eyebrow and twists the corner of his mouth. "That's pretty deep. The only thing that made sense is the heavenly body thing." He eyes my bosom and then winks quick before turning back to the road.

I touch my lip when I remember how he kissed me not so long ago. Kissed me without asking. Imposed his will on me. Showed me his power. Is he toying with me? Does he want to see me scared before he uses that power? Is he savoring the moment? Am *I* savoring the moment?

We drive in silence for I don't know how long. I reach between my legs for water, offering Slay a bottle. He takes it and slides it into that cargo pocket. Eyes still on the road as I play with my hands.

"So you're a vegetarian?" I blurt out when I remember him joking about why he doesn't eat people.

He grins. "That surprise you?"

I smile, sneaking a glance at the slabs of raw muscle that's Slay's chest. "I guess gorillas are vegetarian and they're pretty big and strong."

Slay looks down at himself and frowns. "You making fun of me, Sugar?"

"No!" I say. "I don't make fun of psychos!"

"OK, now I *know* you're making fun of me."

"Hey, you called yourself a psycho first!"

Slay glances up and then grunts. "Guess I did." He shrugs and nods. "Guess I am."

I narrow my eyes at this glistening mountain of vegetarian muscle. "I'm not so sure, actually. Cruelty to animals is one of the earliest signs of a violent psychopath. But you don't even eat animals."

"How do you know I don't torture them just for the hell of it?"

"*Do* you torture animals just for the hell of it?"

Slay's face goes dark with color. "I'd kill any man who does. Actually that was my second kill, come to think of it. I'd just turned eleven, and I saw a couple of street thugs fucking with a baby rat. They'd nailed its tail to a board and were poking it with their knives. Couldn't stand to see it. Something snapped in me, and I just unloaded on them. Killed the first guy with my bare hands. Second guy hauled ass like a leopard was after him." He smiles like the memory is a fond recollection of his childhood. "Took that little critter home with me. He lived with me for the rest of his life—which was only like two years, but still. Never needed a cage. He'd even let me pet him."

I stare, my smile slowly breaking. He is human. Who knew. "What was his name?"

Slay blinks, tapping on the steering wheel and screwing up his face. "Ratty," he says softly.

I double over with a belly-laugh, and I can almost see Slay as an overgrown kid playing with a rat called Ratty. Slay rumbles out a laugh alongside, and his heavy body shakes the entire chassis of the car as he grunts and guffaws mightily.

Then through the shared laughter I hear a small beep. I'm still bent forward, and my heart races when I see that it's my iPhone that I'd tossed on top of my backpack after checking it earlier. It's picked up a signal! Ohmygod, I can call for help! Transmit my location! Summon the cavalry! Tell them about Carl! Ohmygod, it's over!

My laughter turns hollow as I silently tap my phone's emergency call button. I know once I'm connected they'll be able to track my phone. I can't talk, of course, but the 911 operators are trained for that. They'll assume it's a carjacking or kidnapping and send the cavalry.

The call connects and I let the phone slide to the floormats so Slay doesn't hear the faint voice of the operator. I laugh once more for effect and then sit upright. Slay is grinning so wide I almost feel guilty that soon he's going to be handcuffed and on his way to prison. But then I glance at his uniformed pants and I suddenly remember him passing a comment about prison earlier! Oh shit, he just broke out of prison, didn't he? Which means that the authorities are already looking for him. And if I remember my prison-break movies right, a killer-convict on the loose gets a shoot-on-sight order on his head. Maybe even a bounty!

Now the car-radio crackles to life, startling me before I remember leaving it on standby when I couldn't find a station earlier. It must have scanned through again and picked up something!

. . . the fugitive is Slayton Singer, and he's considered armed and extremely dangerous. Federal Marshalls have issued a shoot-on-sight order, and the FBI has already authorized a $75,000 bounty for information leading directly to his capture or death.

"Seventy five grand?" Slay says with a snort. "My head's worth six figures at least. What do you think, Sugar? Ain't I dangerous enough for a six-figure bounty?"

I swallow the lump of guilt and force a tight smile, my fingers curling as I think of that phone transmitting our location. Now it occurs to me that shit, I might even get paid the bounty once the Marshalls catch Slay.

And then I remember that they won't be catching him.

They'll be killing him.

Which means I just phoned in Slay's death warrant.

I just killed him.

"Listen, Slay," I whisper, clasping my hands between my thighs and sliding them towards my phone. I'm more scared now than I ever was, and I tell myself to shut the hell up, that I can't wimp out now, that just because Slay softened up and showed his humanity doesn't mean he's a *good* human. What do you think he'll do to you if he sees that you just betrayed him while laughing like a hyena? Think he'll shrug and say it's all right? Think he'll smile and call you Sugar again? Think he'll—

And then suddenly a vehicle pops up way down the road ahead of us, and Slay slows the car and tightens. I hold my breath, waiting for the lights and sirens to go on. But it's not the cops or US Marshalls, and when I hear Slay curse and make a squealing U-Turn, I realize it's the same black Wrangler with the bandits who took Carl!

"They must have heard about the bounty and doubled back," Slay growls, completing the turn and flooring the gas. The car leaps forward, but almost immediately we see flashing lights and hear the drone of sirens ahead of us! "Fuck, we're boxed in!" Slay roars, his eyes like green slits, the rage making his spit sizzle on his lips. He glances in the rearview at the bandits, and I turn and gasp when I see two of the thugs standing up and taking aim with their assault rifles!

"Out!" Slay shouts, slamming on the brakes. He

leans over and pops my door and then pushes me out just before the bullets crash into the car, riddling the back of the seat with holes the size of my fists!

I scream as I hit the dusty ground, rolling away from the road, screaming again and then coughing up sand and grit as I scramble towards a boulder that's the only cover I see. I crouch and cough again, my breathing so furious I don't think I'm actually getting any oxygen. I shut my eyes tight and try not to have a heart attack, but when I open my eyes to see Slay's big face a foot away from mine, I start to scream and then just gurgle when he clamps his salty hand over my mouth and stares me into submission with those sea-monster eyes.

Beyond the boulder on the road I hear shouts and shots, calls for surrender and howls of *Die, Gringo!* Somewhere in there I think I hear Carl squealing like a piglet, and I'm vaguely relieved to see that he's alive. How much longer he'll be alive is anyone's guess, but hey, we all got problems right now.

"Sometimes two problems are better than just one," Slay grunts as the gunshots thunder through the desert, the shouts rip through the hot air, the sirens wail like background music. He grabs my arm and beckons with his head. "See what you did, Sugar?" He whispers, his eyes shining just enough to send a chill through my spine. His jaw tightens and he licks his lips, staring a hole through my guilty soul. "Don't do that again, Sugar. You hear me, Sugar? Now, you know about the stars and planets and all that shit, right? So you know that every action gets a reaction. Every push gets a pull. Every betrayal comes with retribution."

And then, without another word, Slay grabs me by the back of my neck, heaves me across his lap, and pulls my dusty cargo shorts down so fast I almost pass out with shock! I try to scream, but he muzzles me again and even though I bite his fingers it doesn't matter. I feel his cock throb under my belly as I wriggle on his thighs like a fish on the chopping block. My soft cotton panties are still on, and I'm breathing hard and heavy through my nose as I feel Slay's eyes on my big round ass, sense his hot breath snorting down on my lower back like a bull in heat.

He runs his thumb down my ass, pushing my panties into my crack in the most filthy way. I get that feeling between my legs that makes me think I'm going to get fucked to death out here in the desert. My pussy is so wet I can smell myself in the breeze, and from the way Slay's cock is flexing up against my tummy I know he's fighting a raging need to rip my panties off and take me face-down in the dirt. The thought should terrify me but it doesn't, and it's only now that I realize I should be surprised a man like Slay hasn't already taken me ten times by now.

The air still thunders with gunshots, and the shouts and sirens rip the ether to shreds. But behind this boulder it feels weirdly peaceful. I think about the balance of power between planets and stars, the sun and the moon, how the push and pull of opposites holds the universe together. And now I feel a ripple of power go through me even though I'm at the mercy of a murderer twice my size. I feel powerful because I know there's something in this monster that held him in check, kept him from savaging me like an animal, made him keep that python of a cock tied down instead of unleashing it inside me.

"I was right about you," I mumble into his hand, somehow getting the words out through the cracks in his big crooked fingers. "You're not a murdering maniac with no self control. I bet you can give me a reason for every kill you ever made, Slay. I bet deep down you wouldn't have killed Carl even though he's a disgusting snake who cares only about his

Stranded with the Psycho 55

own ass. You could have taken me twenty times by now and I'd have been powerless to stop you. But you didn't. You haven't. And you won't."

Slay moves under me, and his hand rests flat on my ass, his body tensing up, his breath catching like my words sting. Two stray bullets slam into the other side of the boulder, making the rock hum with resonance. Then, as the boulder still vibrates with the twin gunshots, I feel Slay's hand move off my ass and immediately come back down twice in quick succession!

Smack! Smack! come the open-palmed slaps right on the meat of my ass!

Smack! comes a third!

I scream into his hand, my eyes so wide they almost fly off my head. Slay spanks me a fourth time, making my heavy rear globes tremble as pain screams through me. Then suddenly there's stillness, silence, serenity. Now Slay leans close to my ear, his growly rumble making me almost pee in my panties.

"The first two were for betraying me even after I saved your ass from those banditos." He rubs his palm flat on my stinging ass, his warm breath sending shivers down the curve of my back, his cock digging into my belly button as it gets bigger and harder and more dangerous. "The next two were for thinking you know *anything* about me." He pauses and takes a breath, flexing his cock so hard it almost lifts my body. Then he strikes me again, one tight, swift slap that gets me on both cheeks at once, the sting so clear I can feel his palm branded in red streaks on my quivering ass.

"And what was that last one for?" I whimper through my drool-sticky lips as he takes his hand away and pulls my shorts back up so hard my panties jam deep into my slit.

"That was for me," he whispers, kissing the back of my neck and then jerking me to my feet, grabbing my arm, and gesturing to the open desert. "Come on. We're moving. I think those banditos chased off the cops, which means you got just two choices, Sugar: Ride shotgun with me, or take your chances that the Mexicans sell you to a nice gentleman with a spacious sex-dungeon."

5
__SLAY__

"I changed my mind about the sex dungeon," she says, squinting at me through sunburned eyelids as we trudge through the red desert that's studded with twenty-foot cacti and hardy shrubs that are probably waiting for us to drop dead and decay so our bones can add some calcium to the soil. "Sex dungeons have air-conditioning, don't they?"

"Mine sure as hell will," I grunt, glancing at the shade up her shorts as she leans forward to climb a small hill. The way her ass jiggled when I spanked her still makes me grin—even though grinning's no fun with dry, cracked lips. I squint up at the sun, noticing it getting closer to the horizon. Then I whip my head left and right, scanning the landscape to make sure we aren't getting turned around. That's the reason folks get lost in the desert—everything looks the same in every direction. No landmarks except the sun, which will be gone in a couple of hours. And that could be a problem, since I ain't no sailor who can navigate by the stars.

"You going to build a sex dungeon in Outlaw Town?" she asks, shooting me a sideways look as we get to the crest of the hill and stop for a breather.

"It's *all* sex dungeons in Outlaw Town, Sugar. You'll see."

Sienna swallows hard, blinking and glancing towards the Southeast horizon. She's sitting on a rock, and I stand beside her, arms folded over my bare chest like a gargoyle protecting the goddess. Her words still echo in my head, still swirl through my soul. She said I wasn't a psycho. Nobody's ever said that before.

Not even me.

"Just messing with you, Sugar," I say, forcing myself to speak so I don't have to think. "Outlaw Town's a free-for-all where sex and violence lives out in the open. I'll leave you at the border. There's no real border patrol this far away from a city, but

Stranded with the Psycho 59

there's a gas station where you can call for help. Just wait till I get across to Mexico first, OK?"

Sienna frowns up at me and lets out a fake sigh. "So you're not going to keep me?"

I shift on my feet, my cock moving like an angry snake. "Reinforcements must have arrived at the scene. Cops and Marshalls must have found your rental car, found your stuff. Now they know you're with me, and if they think I've kidnapped a nice American girl, they won't stop looking for me. If I let you go, they won't cross the border to come after me. I become the Mexican police's problem, and that's not a problem in Outlaw Town."

Sienna nods. "Makes sense, I guess." A shrug and she turns away. "I won't take it personally."

I cock my head and my cock's head goes up like it's listening. It does make sense to cut her loose, but I've never been big on doing sensible shit. I just go with my gut mostly—I kill when I'm angry, eat when I'm hungry, and fuck when I'm in the mood. Though I've been in the mood for hours right now but my pants haven't come off yet. What does that mean? Am I losing my edge? What's this girl doing to me? Why is she making me think there might be future for us?

Fucking ridiculous, I tell myself. You're a scarred,

broken killer on the run from the law. There's a bounty on your head and a shoot-to-kill order on your ass. You've never told a woman you loved her, and no woman's ever come close to saying those words to your twisted soul. Your path winds through darkness and violence, and that's the only place you're headed, the only thing in your future. Maybe you sense you're close to the end of the road, Slay. That's why you're getting soft on this chick. That's why you're imagining her big and pregnant with your monster babies. You're facing the abyss and you want to leave your mark on the world, sow your seed like the animal you are. This isn't about her. This is about you. You've lost it, Slay. Lost your edge. Hell, you'll probably be killed within a week in Outlaw Town at this rate.

I force myself to keep talking to stop my spinning mind. "Cops must have seen your boyfriend with the banditos. They'll put out the word for him too. They'll have his info from the car rental papers." My triceps twitch as I think of that sniveling snake who would have sold his own mother to the devil to avoid acting like a man.

"He's not my boyfriend. He's just a boy. Not a man." Sienna's tanned face darkens, her small fists clenching as she glances up at me and then looks away. "A man protects his woman. I know that sounds lame and old-fashioned, but it's how I feel."

"That's how I feel too." I uncross my arms and reach out my big hand. "Come on, Sugar. We got a few more miles to the border. Gotta get there before sundown or else we might get off track."

Sienna takes my hand and I pull her upright so fast she stumbles into me, my flat, hard stomach tensing up as she bounces off me, her face flush.

"We won't get off track in the dark. I'll know where we are just by looking up at the stars." She glances up at me and winks. "Unless you're afraid of the dark. Can't help you there, Psycho."

I laugh, holding her hand which feels small like a child's, soft like a rose, warm like a sunset. We run downhill together like toddlers, giddy and breathless, happy and free. There's a strange energy between us—maybe because she knows I'm going to let her go, that she'll be safe soon, that even her idiot ex will probably escape with his life if not his life savings.

But as we settle into a steady clip, that energy drains from me as the sun begins to set. Because now I see my future again. A future dark and lonely. And for the first time ever I start to think that maybe I am afraid of the dark . . .

Now that I've had a moment of light in my life.

6
SIENNA

"The starlight is so strong in the clear air that I almost have a headache." I stop so I can stare directly up without falling. Slay stops too, but he doesn't look up. He's looking at me, just like he's been doing for like an hour as we walked in silence.

But it was a peaceful silence, I think as I glance at Slay and then point up at Venus, which is bright like a full moon. Almost a melancholy silence, like we both know that in a few hours we'll be going our separate ways forever, that there's no chance in heaven or hell that our paths will ever cross again. We're from two worlds so far apart it's unfathomable that our paths *ever* crossed, in fact!

Though some of those stars are billions of miles apart but yet look like they're joined by some invisible force, I remind myself as I hear Slay breathe beside me like a silent sentry. The night sky looks like a diamond-studded canopy, and I hug myself and smile as the breeze blows cool and gentle, a reprieve from the dryer-hot daytime air. I've been leading us since sunset, and I know we're just a few miles from the border now.

"Where's that cluster-fuck of stars and moons that you came out here to see, Sugar?" Slay looks up and rotates his big body slowly.

I go close to him and point. "There. There. And there. But we aren't in the right spot. You can see it from here just fine, but there's a specific spot that's a focal point for the alignment. A power angle." I shrug sheepishly. "Yeah, yeah. It's New Agey and kinda dumb. But it's based on some old calculations done by the Aztecs."

Slay is silent, still staring. "I'm part Aztec," he says absentmindedly, his gaze fixed on that alignment like he's in a trance. Suddenly he blinks and looks away like it took some effort. "How far is that secret spot?"

I swallow and then glance back up. "Hard to say for sure without a GPS to lock in the coordinates.

But it should be in a straight line thataway, maybe four miles?"

Slay takes a breath. Then he takes my hand. I don't question it. It's out of the way, but somehow it feels like it's very much on our way. Maybe it *is* the way.

"What did the Aztecs do during this alignment?" Slay asks. "Sacrifice a hundred virgins and maybe a goat?"

I chuckle. "They just did that whenever there was a full moon." Slay grins and I continue. "No, the Aztecs actually held mass weddings during this alignment. It was what they called a Star Marriage alignment, where two stars get so close it looks like they're touching. Like they're being joined. United. Married." I glance up at Slay as a weird shudder hits. I feel it in him too. "Of course, it only *looks* like they're touching. They're still millions of miles apart in reality."

Slay glances down at me and grunts. "Sounds about right."

I giggle and loop my arm through his as we walk. I don't know what I'm doing, why I'm acting this way, why I'm *feeling* this way, but I don't question it. I feel like a new person under the stars, in the empty desert, so far from my old life that I barely remember who I am in the straight world, hate the idea of going back to my little New Agey storefront in Tucson. Now I understand why Shamans would come out to the desert for their vision quests—because you really *do* see visions of your future out here, catch glimpses of your true self, the eternal self that's usually buried under the stresses and routines and drudgery of regular life.

What if this *was* my regular life, comes a thought that blazes through me like a shooting star. I glance over at Slay, a shiver going through me when I face that thought I've been avoiding all day, a thought that slithers beneath the surface like a snake in the sand. It's a thought that came to me when Slay kissed me like I was his. It's a thought that whispered inside me when he said he was keeping me.

And it's a thought that almost broke me when he finally told me he'd let me go.

A thought that's so crazy I refuse to think it, so dangerous I refuse to acknowledge it, so terrifying I refuse to accept it.

But yet it lingers like that snake in the sand.

It lingers as we walk hand-in-hand like we're being drawn to that power-spot, that ancient fulcrum of energy, that invisible beam of starlight that comes from two celestial beings joining as one, a

Stranded with the Psycho

wedding between earth and sky, a marriage of heaven and hell, a union of dark and light.

The thought lingers even though I hate it, even though I deny it, even though I can't believe it.

And then I look up and see those two stars joined as one, their union witnessed by a circle of smaller stars. I stop and stare, and Slay stops by my side, his arm sliding around my waist. We both look up at the same time, and I swear those stars just looked back at us, their light reflecting ours, their energy raising ours past all considerations of common sense and reason, ignoring any thoughts of what's right or wrong, what's decent or decadent, what *should* happen versus what's really happening.

And as I look over at Slay, see the starlight in his green eyes, see behind the veil of his violence, I come face to face with the gentleness in his soul, a soul that was twisted by violence but somehow still grew straight and true, still led him to this place, still led him to me.

Now I let that dangerous thought come, and when it comes I feel its truth, feel its power, feel its force.

You're his, whispers the thought. You're his.

And then, as those two star-lovers kiss each other in the heavens, Slay pulls me close and leans in low and kisses me here on earth, in this cosmic low-ground that's a reflection of what's above, this arena where dark and light must always live in balance, where one cannot be seen without the other, he kisses me.

By God, he kisses me.

7
SLAY

The kiss is nothing like the first kiss and nothing like any kiss. I don't know if there's something to this power-space New Age crap, but I do know there's something in the way her warm lips feel against mine, the way her heart beats in time with mine, they way our breath swirls and eddies in the dark night like tiny dust-devils playing with each other.

I don't know where the kiss came from, and I don't know why she's kissing me back. Hell, I don't know anything anymore, it feels. Nothing more than this is a once-in-a-lifetime moment for me just like it is with those stars above us.

"I may not be able to keep you, Sugar," I whisper, stroking her sun-streaked face and kissing her on the nose and then the lips again before pulling back so I can look at her beauty. "But I'm gonna keep this memory forever. Forever, you hear?"

"Me too," Sienna whispers as I kiss her again. "Though it feels like a dream, Slay."

"Better than a nightmare," I grunt through a wet smile. Fuck, she makes me feel like I'm not a bad man, not a forsaken soul, not an outcast destined to spend the rest of my life running or hiding like a hunted dog. Of course, I am all those ugly things, but that doesn't matter tonight. Tomorrow I'll face the lonely nightmare of my life. Tonight I'll enjoy my dream.

So I devour Sienna's lips with an urgency I feel in my bones, jamming my tongue into her mouth and rolling it around so I can taste her sweetness, swallow her essence like it's a magic potion that will get me into heaven though I belong in hell. My arms slide around her back, my hands moving down along her curves and resting on her ass. I squeeze hard, almost lifting her curvy body off the ground, and she whimpers and then gasps when my cock flexes against the front of her shorts.

I reach between us and rub her crotch with the

back of my hand, and she groans and grinds into my knuckles, the heat of her mound warming my skin through her shorts. I kiss her hard and raw as I unzip her and yank her fly open so I can get my hand in there. Her warm wetness coats my fingers through her soaked panties, and her scent is so strong in the dry cool night that I drop to my knees in a flash, pulling her shorts and panties down in one swift motion.

"Oh, shit, Slay," she groans as I slam my face between her thighs, my mouth open wide, tongue driving hard, sliding stiffly all the way into her cunt and curling as I dig my fingers into her buttcheeks.

Sienna grabs my hair and holds on like a little monkey as I tongue-fuck her so deep she's dripping down the sides of my mouth, all the way down my neck. Her feminine musk is thick like an animal's, and the heavy scent of her sexual secretions mixed with the day's sweat and a hint of salty-sweet tang is like a filthy drug that makes me want to eat her up, swallow that pussy whole, drink her dry and then howl at the stars, beat my chest at the moon, stare down the sun until it looks away in defeat.

She's pulling my hair so hard it hurts, and I pull back for a hot breath and grin when I glance up and see her face twisted in a grimace of ecstasy so profound I know she's in that place where dreams and nightmares are the same fucking thing. I keep smiling as my gaze travels down her tank-top which is hanging off her shoulder, her big left breast dark and poignant in the night.

I massage her ass as I suckle her dark nipple like a filthy wolfcub at the teat, groaning as her areola pricks up in my mouth. Slowly I part her rear cheeks as I drag her black top off her other shoulder with my teeth, and I touch my middle finger to her asshole just as I take her other boob into my mouth and suck so hard she almost collapses.

"Oh, *fuck*, Slay!" she cries as I circle her rear rim and then drag my tongue down along her center-line, down past her belly-button, back to that dark triangle of musky curls that hide her crescent moon that's wet and red and mine, all mine.

For tonight, at least.

Sienna comes all over my nose and mouth as I bury myself in her bush, and she tastes so sweet and pure I groan and gasp and drink deep and long. Then I pull her left leg over my shoulder to spread her wider, and I get under there and drive my tongue into her pussy at the same time pushing my middle finger into her ass.

She screams and pulls my hair hard enough to

scalp me, and I howl as she squirts down on me and then rides my tongue like a cowgirl of the old west. I take her juice and let her ride my face through her climax, and then I'm on my feet and unleashing my cock as my balls thunder for a release that will rival that of a sandstorm.

Sienna sways on her feet as I let go of her long enough to rip these infernally small pants off my powerful thighs, and when my cock springs out big and thick like a cactus swollen and gorged, she gasps and swoons, her eyes going wide like she understands how fucking aroused I am for her, how badly I need her, how deep I'm going to take her.

"I got you, Sugar," I whisper, grabbing her around the waist as she sways again. "Up you go."

I lift her off her feet, cradling her like a child as I carry her to a smooth, flat rock that looks like it was placed there for us. Those stars are bright like headlamps, and as I move with her in my arms I get the sense that all the stars are alive and watching, witnessing our love like *we're* the once-in-a-lifetime event, our union mirroring the one happening above us.

We're at the rock, and I step up onto it without thinking and immediately gasp when I feel that star-power like it's a real thing. Now I look up, holding Sienna in my arms like a virgin offering to the Aztec god. My ancient blood stirs as Sienna stares up at her precious star-marriage, and when she turns her gaze to me I see those stars reflected in her brown eyes and I understand what she means about how this will be remembered as a dream, not a memory.

My heart fills with a warmth that's new to me, and for one magical moment that heat chases away the coldness that's lived in me ever since I was old enough to witness the horrors of the world. For that one magical moment I am forgiven instead of forsaken, loved instead of feared, happy instead of hateful.

"Is this what love feels like?" I mutter, not sure if I'm speaking to Sienna or myself or to the empty desert.

"I feel it too, Slay," Sienna whispers, her arms looped around my thick neck as we hover on that rock altar. "And now I understand why it can only be this way, a once-in-a-lifetime thing. This much power can't sustain itself for more than one moment in time."

"You talking about the stars or us?"

"Is there a difference? Doesn't feel like it right now," she whispers. "You know that every particle in the universe—including our bodies—came from an exploding star. Star power is real, Slay. It's in us. That's what we're feeling. I think. I don't know. Oh, shit, I don't know, Slay!"

"I don't know either," I growl, leaning in and touching my nose to hers. "Fuck, if only I could keep you, Sugar. Make you mine forever, not just one night."

She's about to say something, but I shut her up with a kiss. I see the little voice in her head that wants to believe we can be something, and I won't let that voice get any louder. She's a straight girl from the straight world having a wild experience out here in the desert. She's had a crazy day and she needs this release as much as I do. But that's all it can be. I can't really keep her even though I yearn to do just that. I can't keep her. This is my test, the universe seeing if I'll cross a line I never have, swore I never would. My first kill was to protect a girl who couldn't protect herself. The kills after that . . . yeah, Sienna's right: There was a reason for each one. Whether the reason was good or not is for the Great Spirit to decide when my bones turn to dust.

"Then keep me," she whispers as our noses touch again and our lips touch again and I swear our hearts touch too. "Keep me, Slay."

We kiss again, and my vision blurs even as that dream becomes clearer. But life with me can never be a dream, and if there's a shred of my soul still pure, I need it to step up and make sure I release this girl, send her back to her safe, normal life, take nothing but the memory of this night with me to my nightmare.

"You got no idea what a life in Outlaw Town is like, what a life on the run would be like, Sugar. I ain't no millionaire Mafioso with Swiss bank accounts and shit," I whisper, rubbing her neck and fisting her hair as the stars watch us. "As magical as this feels right now, it would turn ugly the moment you see we'd be living like rats. One night under the stars with me might be heaven, Sugar, but a lifetime with me would be the kind of hell that'd make the demons scream for mercy."

"I'm not scared of demons," she says, glancing up at the night sky and then back into my eyes. "I'm made of starlight."

"That you are, Sugar," I say, swallowing hard like there's something in my throat. "You even taste like a star."

And I smother her lips again, shutting her mouth and my mind at the same time. I can't take her with me. She knows it and I know it.

But maybe she can take a part of me with her.

Yeah, I think as I sit my bare ass down on the warm rock and carefully position my sugar-sweet starlight spirit-dancer above my ramrod-straight cock that's pointing true north like the Dog Star. Maybe I send a part of me with her, shoot my starlight into her supernova, our once-in-a-lifetime moment spawning a new life.

A new life, comes the thought as I lower Sienna onto my cock, feel her body shudder as my cockhead parts her slit and enters her dark hole, all the way in, all the way deep, all the way home.

8
SIENNA

My home is in the stars, comes the nonsensical thought as Slay lowers me onto his cock and my weight takes him in so deep I can feel him in my throat. A guttural groan emerges from my burning, wet lips, and for a shuddering moment I sit still on Slay, his big hands on my sides, the entire length of his monstrous cock inside me.

He kisses my face—every square inch of my face: forehead and nose and eyelids and cheeks and chin and everything in between. I feel my wet skin glow silver as I smile, feel my vagina flow warm as I moan. Slay is thick like a pillar inside me, and when he flexes I arch my head back and call out like a she-wolf as ecstasy roars up along my center-line, up along my ass and lower back and between my shoulder blades and into my heart.

And then Slay digs his fingers into my thighs and lifts me, dropping me back onto his cock and raising me off again. My eyes roll up in my head as I plunge my nails into his shoulders, and then Slay goes faster, lifting me and bringing me down, again and again, faster and faster until he's bouncing me on his cock like I'm a little girl.

"Oh, hell, Slay," I groan, licking my lips and gasping as I ride this monster's cock like I just rode his tongue. I feel so free and wild out here that I'm almost scared of losing my mind. But then I decide that if this is madness, then fuck it—give me madness!

Slay gives it to me deep and hard again, and now he's rising up as he brings me down, his powerful bull-like haunches ramming upwards so hard my boobs quiver and my teeth rattle and my eyelids flutter. I feel his heavy balls slapping up against my wet undersides with every violent thrust, and I gasp at how my wicked pussy is clenching and releasing and clenching again like it's coaxing Slay's semen up from those massive balls.

"I'm going to come inside you, Sugar," he growls

against my chest, where he's licking the tender space between my boobs which are raw and red from his pinches and bites. "I need to feel myself explode in you, Sienna. Please, babe. I'm so damned close. Oh fuck, your cunt is so warm, so tight, so damned . . . oh hell, oh shit, oh *fuck*!"

And Slay *slams* me down on his cock and *explodes* inside me, his semen erupting like a geyser breaking through the bedrock, filling me so fast he's pouring out of me even as he pumps more of his heat into me. And suddenly my own climax roars in from below, whipping up through me from the head of Slay's cock, from the heat of his seed. Now I'm howling like a hurricane, wailing like the wind, screaming like a siren as Slay yells and shouts and pulls my hair and slaps my sides. He bounces me up and down with a rabid fury, clawing at my ass and fingering my rear hole deep and hard as he takes my left breast into his wide mouth, almost sucking the entire darned thing like he wants to devour me.

We come together naked under the stars, with me shrieking and Slay shouting, our cries of ecstasy rolling across the empty desert, being recorded in the sharp spines of the cacti, in the dry dirt of the land. Finally Slay tenses up and groans as he squeezes out of the last of his load, and then he falls back on the flat rock and pulls me down onto his broad body, keeping his cock inside me, his thick legs intertwined with mine, my hair open and wild, my eyes suddenly wide like an owl's, vision vivid like in those dreams where you're half awake and can't move.

My head spins as I feel Slay's seed move inside me like the living things they are, seeking their place in my body just like we're all seeking our places in the world. I listen to Slay's powerful heart pound steady like a marching drum, and I glance up at his jutting jawbone, those iridescent green eyes, those scars that somehow feel as ancient as the stars. Now I remember what he said right before coming inside me, but instead of panicking I just smile and kiss his hard chest. I understand it. My body understands it. My soul understands it. My brain, not so much—but we'll worry about that later . . . when it's too late to do anything about it.

"Sienna, listen," Slay mutters as he looks down at me nuzzling into his chest. But he doesn't say anything else, instead kissing my head and holding me tighter in his bearlike arms.

"I hear you," I whisper, smiling when I realize we can't talk about what just happened, about that moment of deep longing that this cold, scarred, forsaken monster experienced when he came inside me. I heard it in his voice . . . heard that ancient yearning for a man to leave a part of himself behind, a trace that he once walked the earth, that he shared in that most basic of dances: The Dance of Life.

We lie together as the constellations continue their slow march across the sky, and although the night is cool we're both warm like a hearth on our rock-altar under the spotlight of the stars. Eventually the red glow of dawn shines on our interlocked toes, and Slay kisses my forehead and brushes away a stiff, dust-caked strand of my hair before we both sit up.

Slay dresses me in silence as the sun slowly rises, and the gentle touch of his rough fingers makes me shiver as he pulls up my panties, rubs my pussy, and then with a sigh helps me step into my cargo shorts that are stained red from the dirt. Carefully Slay sucks each of my nipples before pulling my dusty tank-top down. Then he rises and leans past me to grab his pants.

His broad shadow falls over me as I sit with my thighs together on the rock. Slay is semi-hard, and his long brown cock shines gold in the morning light. I reach out and touch it, running my fingers along the shaft and gasping when he goes erect and upright immediately. He grunts and tosses his pants away, standing still like a statue and touching my hair. I slowly jerk him back and forth, cup his heavy balls, and then finally bring my sunchapped lips to his shining red cockhead.

"Damn, Sugar," he groans as I take him into my mouth. He squares his hips and then holds my shoulders, slowly pushing himself down my throat before gripping my head and groaning.

I slide back and forth, my throat open all the way for his length. He's so thick my lips are stretched as wide as they'll go, and when he grips my hair and starts to fuck me in the mouth, I gag and gurgle but somehow hang on.

The sun is warm on my bare neck as I suck Slay, and the wind is gentle and fragrant with the scent of cactus blooms. I catch a glimpse of our shadows, long and otherworldly, like two strange beings moving back and forth, up and down, in and out.

Slay comes quickly in my mouth, groaning and digging his fingers into my shoulders as he pours himself down my throat. I swallow as he finishes, massaging his balls and then looking up at his twisted, happy face. He pants and groans again before pulling out, his cock trailing a thick rope of semen and saliva as I wipe my mouth and blush under my tan.

"Gonna be hard to forget you, Sugar," he whispers, pulling me to my feet and kissing me on my sticky lips. He squeezes my ass and runs the back of his hand along my crotch, and then with a sigh steps away and grabs his pants.

"Maybe I'll come visit," I say as he checks his gun and pulls out the bottle of water he'd stashed in his cargo pocket and which pretty much got us through yesterday. There's maybe three sips left, and he takes one and hands me the rest.

"You can test out my sex dungeon," he says with a wink as I finish the last of our water. We're not far from the border gas station now, but one look at the sun and I know we can't delay much longer. We're already dehydrated, and we need to end this vision quest and walk back to the straight world before the straight world issues the grim reminder that although we're made of stardust, without water we'll be just plain old dust.

And so I place my hand in Slay's, and we walk towards the end of the road.

9
SLAY

"**E**nd of the road, Sugar."

I stop at the summit of a rocky red hill and pull Sienna close. The border is unmarked this far out, but the single-pump gas station is right where it used to be. Good, because we're nearing the danger zone with dehydration. I can see it in Sienna's lips, feel it in her tongue when we kiss with a thirst for each other that I know is our bodies searching for a drink.

"Just in time," Sienna says. "Was getting close to chewing on a cactus pod."

I grin. "You can eat the fruit of a Prickly Pear in a pinch. But stay away from the other cacti. That shit will dehydrate you faster than the sun."

"I know." Sienna pulls on my arm, a cracked smile on her sunstreaked face, red dirt caked in her hair. I've never seen anything so beautiful. Why aren't I keeping her? Oh, right. Redemption or salvation or some crap like that. Fuck, I wish I were a worse man. I wish I really could keep her in a sex dungeon. Maybe that's happening in some other dimension.

Lucky bastard, that other-dimensional Slay is, I think as we pick up the pace now that the thirst skyrockets with the prospect of being quenched.

Though I'm a lucky bastard too, I remember as I cast a sly glance at the cute roundness of Sienna's belly. I try to forget that wild yearning, that primal desperation, that dominant desire to put my seed in her last night. It's best to forget it, I think. Could drive a man crazy to think about something like that. Come tomorrow this girl will be back in her safe, secure world where everyone stops at traffic lights and people tip their hats and say hello or some shit. Even if she does get pregnant, what are the chances she'll decide to keep it? To give birth to the bastard child of a convicted killer? Hah! This chick isn't the serial-killer-groupie type. This was just a one-night stand in the end. Sure, it was the *craziest* one-night-stand in the history of romance, but that don't change what it is.

The gas station looms big as we approach, and

when I see Sienna's relieved smile, I know I was right. She's already looking forward to going back to her world, taking a warm bath, cleaning the dust off her face, soaping her pussy to get the smell of Slay out.

"I got money," she says, digging into her back pocket and pulling out some crumpled bills. "My treat."

I hang back away from the door so the attendant doesn't see me. No doubt the cops and Marshalls put out the word with this guy. Well, I hope they have, I think as I scan the horizon and listen for the sounds of engines. If not, they might be rolling in here any moment with my face on a reward poster.

Now I almost *hope* I hear an engine—the cops, Marshalls, banditos, anyone! It'll delay what I'm dreading: Letting Sugar go back to her world of light while I crawl to my cave of darkness. I shift on my feet and clench my fists, savoring the prospect of having to grab Sienna as a fake-hostage so the cops don't gun me down. It's less than a mile to the border, and although taking an American hostage to Mexico probably means they won't give up the trail, they still won't follow me across the border without calling the Mexican police first. I'd be able to get far enough to get a head start.

A faint smile stretches my lips as my imagination stretches the boundaries of possibility, and when Sienna emerges with two large bottles of ice-cold water that make me pant, I'm relieved to be interrupted before I get beyond the point of letting her go.

"Don't drink it all at once," I caution her as she starts to gulp. "It'll be a shock to the system."

She keeps drinking, her eyes on me as I smile and sigh and take a big sip. "I think my system can handle a few shocks after last night," she whispers, wiping her mouth and swigging that water again until it's gone.

I grin, glancing around again but seeing nothing but stoic cacti watching us like tombstones. "They got my poster up in there yet?"

She blinks, her eyes softening as she nods. "The guy behind the counter is drunk off his ass, though," she says with fake cheer. "I wouldn't worry."

"I'm not worried," I say, rubbing my sunburned neck and then squinting at the road to Mexico. "But I should probably cross the border before anyone pulls up here. Don't want to have to take you hostage, Sugar."

Sienna shrugs, swinging her shoulders and smiling like we're in a high-school playground. "You can take me hostage. I can scream real loud."

I chuckle even though it's hard to laugh with a lump the size of a boulder in my throat. I touch her hand, my knuckles grazing her wrist. I want to pull her into me and kiss her so hard my mouth-print stays on her like a scar. But I don't want someone coming up the road to see us embracing. It might complicate things for her. Hell, it might complicate things for me too. The feds aren't above using leverage to get a fugitive to surrender.

"Hey, let me give you my full name and number," she says, biting her lip and patting her pockets. "I can get a pen and paper from inside. I'll be right—"

"No," I say, grabbing her wrist and saying it again before I think about it and break down like a schoolboy. "No. It's better this way. This way I can't find you. Trust me, Sugar. It's better this way. There's no telling where a man's mind can go if he's having a dark day, Sugar. You're protected better this way."

She sticks her thumbs in her pockets and tries to pout cutely but I see that she's fighting back tears. "I feel protected with you, Slay. What am I going to do back home? How am I going to sit with a straight face in my little store and read someone's star-chart, tell someone where their destiny lies when I just turned my back on my own fate?"

I turn my face to the sun, closing my eyes and

asking the Sun God for strength to do something my mind knows is right even though my body fucking hates it. "We found our fate last night in the desert, Sienna. And it'll stay in the desert. Stay in that moment. Stay recorded in the stars." I place my hand on her chest, just above her breasts. "Our fate will stay in here, Sugar. I'll carry last night with me forever, and that's more than a beast like me deserves." I swallow hard, my gaze flicking down to her belly and then quickly back up to her moist eyes. "And you'll carry . . ." I mutter, trailing off as I push that thought away before it makes me do something that will destroy this sweetheart's life. Outlaw Town isn't a place for a girl like Sienna, and it sure as fuck ain't a place to raise a kid. It's a place where bad men go to disappear.

Where bad men go to die.

Die alone.

And so I touch her smooth cheek and turn my head to the road. I can't say another word, and I can't look into that sweet round face again. This is the end, I tell myself as I take the first step away, my legs feeling like cinderblocks chained to the ground.

But soon I find my footing, and although it's torture like I've never felt, I walk away without turning to look at Sienna again. I do it slow, my ears pricked for the sound of the cops or Marshalls or FBI . . .

some sign from the universe that I shouldn't walk away from Sugar, that we found each other by fate, were drawn together by destiny, were married last night under the blessing of the stars.

But there's no sound but the dry whistle of the desert wind, and with three more lumbering steps I cross the border, cross the line, step over the edge, away from the light and into the dark, away from last night's dream and into today's nightmare.

10
ONE WEEK LATER
SIENNA

"It's a nightmare, I know," I say softly over the phone to Carl's mother. "The FBI is working with the Mexican police. They'll find him. But you said one of the accounts he held jointly with you just got cleaned out, right? So that means he's still alive. That means there's hope. They'll find him. He won't die. He doesn't deserve to die." I sigh as she rails on about if I remember anything else that might help, anything I forgot to tell the cops or feds during three days of interrogation about Slay and Carl and what I was doing out there and how I got away.

Finally I hang up and stare out the window of my little storefront in downtown Tucson. I don't know why I even keep this place since most of my business is done online and via video-chat. Maybe I just like getting out of the house, dressing up and pretending like I'm doing something, like my life is going somewhere.

I frump my face and slouch in my chair, trying not to think about Slay and that night under the stars. I know it was a once-in-a-lifetime moment that was heightened by action and danger, but it's like something changed that night and now I can't be satisfied in this mundane world. It's like I'm a goldfish who spent a day in the open river and then got tossed back in its lonely bowl. What am I going to do here? Find another man like Carl and settle down?

A flash of guilt goes through me when I realize I'm not thinking about Carl at all. If not for his mother calling me constantly like I'm his wife and keeper, I might have forgotten about him completely by now! Is that wrong? Am I horrible? Do I belong in Outlaw Town too?

A chill of excitement goes through me as I glance at my laptop and the search results from the dark-web browser that I managed to figure out. There was nothing about an "outlaw town" on the regular web, but once I got on the Dark Web I read stories about what goes on there.

It really is a Sin City out of urban myth, secluded and self-sufficient, with an underground river providing fresh water for drinking and irrigation and livestock in the surrounding lands. Inside it's a community of criminals, some of them living in walled mansions, others fighting for survival on the streets. It's a free-for-all, where the strong thrive and the weak disappear. Natural selection in its most brutal form. Its most efficient form.

I fantasize sometimes about driving down there, but then my heart beats so fast I have to force myself to think of something calming just to get my head straight. Other times I go through phases where I'm pissed at Slay for saying he's gonna keep me and then walking away like a lone hero who has to sacrifice himself or some lame-ass shit like that. A hero doesn't leave his woman behind, I tell myself through a frumpy pout.

"Well, that's because he's not a hero, he's a psycho, you dumb peanut," I scold myself. "Now let it go. Let him go. Let yourself go . . . go on with life."

But I don't want to go on with this humdrum hamster-wheel of an existence, and I sigh again as I push my phone absentmindedly. Then I jump back when the phone vibrates like it just came alive, and I laugh out loud at my own stupidity. Still laughing I answer it without looking at the number. I'm up for talking to anyone right now, even a telemarketer.

"Wait, *Carl*? Is that you?!" I snap to attention when I hear his peaked voice come through crackling static that feels like a phone call from the outer reaches of the galaxy. "Where are you? Did they let you go? Ohmygod, your parents are *so* worried! Did you call your mom yet? Should I conference her in?"

"Just shut up and listen," Carl says with high-pitched urgency. "I need you to come get me, Sienna."

"Um, sure. Of course. Where are you? Bus station or something?"

"No, I'm in fucking Mexico, Sienna!" he wails. "Those crooks made me clean out all my bank accounts over the week, and finally they agreed to let me go. But I'm in some creepy town in Mexico. It's all fucking criminals here, Sienna! No cops! Just murderers and thieves! I have no money and no one speaks English. Some guy finally let me use his phone—after searching my damned pockets to try and rob me—and I called the US police and they fucking told me I'd have to call the *Mexican* Police to escort me to the border before they can bring me home! Can you believe that?!" Carl pants, his voice going in and out like he's outside and looking around. "And no way in hell I'm trusting the

Mexican Police. Fuck, they're in cahoots with those guys who took me! We stopped at a checkpost and the cops just grinned at me and patted my cheeks and called me an American pig who will make a fine bacon!"

I cover my mouth to hide my giggle, and then I clear my throat even though my head is far from clear. For some reason I'm excited about the prospect of driving down there, even if it's just to pick Carl up from the outskirts of Outlaw Town. Somewhere in the back of my mind I'm hoping I'll see Slay strolling down the street, a Sombrero on his head, eye-patch on his face, dead chicken dangling from his big hand. Oh, wait. He's a vegetarian.

"On my way," I say cheerfully like I'm heading down to the mall. There should be a hundred other options to get Carl out of there, but if the US authorities can't do anything in Mexico and Carl's too afraid to call the Mexican cops, what else can I do? Tell Carl's Mom to drive down there? I owe Carl that much, don't I? After all, the trip was my idea. Yeah. I should go. I have to go.

I *want* to go.

11
OUTLAW TOWN, MEXICO
TWELVE HOURS LATER
SIENNA

I want to go so bad I have to cross my legs at the thigh to keep from wetting myself. But I can see the lights of Outlaw Town over the next hill, and I can stop to pee on my way back across the border once I've got Carl.

"Let's see . . ." I mutter, glancing at the map I printed out from the Dark Web. Carl said he'd wait near the edge of town, under a lighted billboard for Juan Cabrero Tequila. I'd asked if he meant Jose Cuervo, but he insisted it was Juan Cabrero. "Huh. What do you know? It *is* Juan Cabrero."

The billboard comes up on my left as I roll my

red Saturn rental car down the hill. The ad has a distinguished mustachioed man with a pirate's hat. "Looks like an ad for rum, not tequila," I say absentmindedly as I glance down the road, towards the gaudy lights of Outlaw Town, my eyes straining in the vague hopes of seeing Slay. My bladder squeals as I slow the car down, and I decide with relief that I'm going to drive into town after picking up Carl. Find a bathroom. Maybe find my forever. After all, it has to be fate that I'm back here, right? Of course it's fate. Destiny. Meant-to-be. My happily ever after.

Now I see a shadowy figure beneath the looming billboard, and suddenly all the doubts I'd successfully ignored earlier come screaming back. I should have brought someone with me. I should have brought a gun. What the hell was I thinking driving down here alone, setting myself up to be kidnapped—this time without Slay to save my ass by showing everyone his prison tattoos!

"Ohmygod, this is *so* stupid, *so* dumb, *so* wrong," I say out loud as I inch closer and see that it is indeed Carl, his clothes torn and dirty, face bruised but not broken. I glance past him to see if there's anyone else around, thugs hiding in the shadows, banditos crouched behind hillocks. Why would they let Carl go here, I start to think as I pull to a stop and try to smile as Carl comes scampering up, his eyes wide and wild, his gait loping and unstable.

"Open up!" he shouts, rapping on the window and glaring at me. "For fuck's sake, Sienna! Unlock the fucking—"

I click open the locks, shifting in my seat as I keep watch for a trap. But there's no one on the street, no movement in the scrubland. Carl gets in and buckles up, and I'm glad he doesn't try to hug me or heaven forbid kiss me. We're still broken up, far as I'm concerned.

"Water? Food?" I say, popping the divider between the seats. "Wow, Carl, I'm so glad you—"

And I stop talking. I just stare.

"Take a left up there," Carl says, his voice so tense I feel it cut through me. He gestures with the small silver handgun that's pointing right at my side. It's cocked and looks loaded, and immediately I know I'm the dumbest girl in the world . . . and Carl is probably the dumbest guy.

"Carl, are you crazy?" I whisper, keeping the car at a crawl. "What did you do? What deal did you make with those guys?"

Carl glances out the front as we approach the city limits. Then he turns to me and shrugs. "They were going to kill me, Sienna. I offered them anything. They just laughed and said I had nothing left to offer." He swallows hard and shrugs nervously. "So I offered them . . . you."

I blink and shake my head in small, jerking movements like a bird. "You fucking idiot, Carl. You brought me down here so you could . . . what . . . *trade* me for yourself? Forget how *wrong* that is for a second and think about how *stupid* it is! You think they're going to let you live? Carl, you just killed *both* of us, you epic loser of a man!"

I glance into his eyes, hoping to see a flicker of recognition that our best chance is to make a run for it. But my heart sinks when I see the resignation in his blue eyes that are faded to dishwater gray. I know how Carl thinks. He knew that if he didn't offer me, he'd be dead anyway. This way at least there's a *chance* they let him go. So basically he traded my life for a teeny, tiny chance that he doesn't get killed too. What a man he is.

And what a dumb cow I am. Driving down here like it was a trip to Disneyland. Hoping I'd see Slay or something lame like that. What was I thinking? What was I—

Now I gasp when that black Jeep rumbles onto the road and cuts me off. Two banditos leap out, rifles pointed at the windshield. Suddenly I see one of the rifles spit fire, and then I scream when two bullets crash through the glass, both shots hitting Carl right in the chest!

I'm still screaming when the banditos pull me out of the car, and I kick out wildly as I wail into the night, call to the stars to save my dumb ass, to make good on the promise they made to us that once-in-a-lifetime night.

12
THE NEXT MORNING SLAY

My eyes are bloodshot and my head woozy. I don't sleep at night no more. Every night I'm up on the roof of the little hacienda where I rent a room on credit. Every night I'm staring at the stars like a lost sailor who doesn't know how to find his way home.

I stroll to the edge of the flat roof terrace and put my hands on my hips as I glance down. Three stories up. Jumping from here is neither here nor there. I grunt and step back, stretching my arms out wide and cracking my knuckles just by tightening my sledgehammer-sized fists.

"What the fuck's going on there?" I mutter,

squinting as I see a crowd gathering at the market square. Mostly men—but then this entire fucking town is mostly men. The only women here are the ones for sale—either willingly or not.

And that's what's being sold in this early morning meat market, I realize with a disinterested grunt. I don't get involved in that kind of business—not as a customer or a crusader. In this town you live and let live . . . or else you die. You want to live in hell, then you gotta ignore the demons. You gotta remind yourself that you're one of hell's monsters too.

Still, I can't help but stare at the crowd as the auction begins. I can't see the girls from up here, but something in me *wants* to see the girls today. I haven't touched a whore since I got down here, and I don't know if I'll ever touch a woman again after having Sienna. I don't want to spoil the taste of her lips in my mouth. Don't want to taint my soul that stole a slice of salvation by walking away from her.

"But that don't mean I can't look," I say as I head down the metal ladder and stroll to the marketplace. By the time I get there the crowd is ten deep, but my height makes these guys feel like elves at my feet, and I stand front and center, square my shoulders, and with a sigh and a headshake take a look at the depravity of the world I now live in.

And my eyes almost burst out of my head when I see what I see.

Sienna.

My Sienna.

Sweet like sugar. Delicate like a doll. Scared like a child.

And without even stopping to think, I raise my hand and snap my fingers at the auctioneer. I point at Sienna, and when the auctioneer calls out the standing bid, I gesture with my thumb to up it, and then I nod and push my way through the crowd to seize my prize.

When she sees me she swoons on her feet, her face drooping and her eyes rolling and her knees buckling and her body swaying.

But she doesn't fall, because I'm there to catch her.

"Hang on, Sugar," I whisper into her hair as I lift her into my arms like a little girl. "I got you. I got you, Sugar. I got you, and this time I really am keeping you."

She murmurs something and stirs, and I kiss her lips and bring forth her sweet smile. The crowd parts for me as I carry her past their gaping maws, and although I'm smiling at the way fate wound its way back and tossed us together again, we're not *quite* at our forever yet.

Because I have twenty-four hours to pay what I bid . . .

And I ain't got the fucking money.

13
EIGHT HOURS LATER
SIENNA

"That's all of my money," I say as I hand Slay a thick envelope as we walk past whirring washing machines and spinning dryers. "So that Laundromat is also a bank. Interesting. Thank heavens for wire transfers."

Slay glances at the cash, and then he grunts and looks away, his face tight, his eyes narrowed.

"What?" I say with a frown. He doesn't answer, and finally I stop on the sunny sidewalk and put my hands on my hips and glare. "Ohmygod, are you pissed that you had to get the money to pay for me from . . . me? Is your freakin' male pride hurt?"

Slay shrugs. "Where I come from, a man pays for his own sex slave," he grunts, walking stiff and straight.

"Sex slave?" I say, catching up to him and linking my arm with his as a hunchback with an eye-patch peers at us with his good eye. "Does that mean you've already built the sex dungeon?"

"Working on it," Slay says, finally breaking a smile and kissing me on the nose. "For now I'll just chain you to the radiator."

I close one eye and frown up at him. "Why do they have radiators in the desert?"

Slay grins. "They don't work. We just use them for anchoring the chains so our sex slaves don't escape."

"I won't escape," I whisper through a smile as we stroll through the town of murderers and madmen, a world which feels every bit as exciting as Disneyland when you're protected by someone who's also a murderer and a madman. "I'm here to stay, Slay."

He looks down at me, bites his lip, and then nods, his green eyes trying to hide the joy I feel in his soul.

"You don't got no choice but to stay, Sugar," he growls. "Coz this time I really am keeping you. Keeping you forever, Sugar. Keeping you till we turn back to stardust."

And then he kisses me as a street sweeper with a dead chicken in his hand mutters something and drags his broomstick around us.

A murderer, I think as I kiss him back.

A madman, I shudder as he grabs my ass in this lawless land.

And mine, I sigh as I arch my neck back and swear I can feel the stars smiling behind the veil of sunlight.

Yup, mine.

Mine always.

Mine forever.

∞

EPILOGUE
FIVE YEARS LATER
SLAY

"Who would have thought murderers and madmen like to get their starcharts done?" Sienna says sweetly, strolling through our sprawling hacienda that's got a well-monitored fence and ample grounds for the kids and dogs to play. It's an oasis of light within the darkness of this town, and I wouldn't have it any other way. This is who we are. No sense trying to fight it.

"You did," I say, winking at our five year old twins Sirius and Saturnia.

They roll their green eyes at us. They've heard this routine before: Sienna reminding me that she's the one who started a business in Outlaw Town, bringing in a stable income while I do shady jobs for the occasional infusion of big money. We've been a dynamite team, and although I didn't think we could raise good kids in hell, my angel of light saw to it that we did exactly that.

"My *pregnant* angel of light," I add as I pull her onto my lap and squeeze her milky breasts as the twins snicker and look away. Although I wouldn't fuck mama ass-up on the dinner table with the kids around, we don't hide the physical side of love from them.

But neither do we hide the spiritual side of love, I think as Sienna pulls away to take a video-call from a nervous loanshark who's wondering how many of the guys that owe him money will get killed for some other outlawish reason before they pay him back. I snicker when Sugar politely explains she isn't that kind of stargazer.

Of course, I always see stars when I gaze at her, I think as she cradles her baby-bulge and kisses the twins and then saunters over to me. Outside the dogs bark at the sun, the birds sing from the trees, and we smile from our Garden of Eden nestled in the bowels of hell. A fairytale dream hiding in the folds of a nightmare.

But it's our nightmare.

And our dream.

And only when you put them together do you get the balance that keeps the universe going, keeps the moons smiling, keep the stars shining.

Shining forever.

Always and forever.

∞

FROM THE AUTHOR

Thanks so much for reading!
Hope you had fun with Slay and Sienna!

The CURVY FOR KEEPS Series rages on with another wild one: WIFED BY THE WARLORD!

And do consider some of my other super-hot stuff: DRAGON'S CURVY MATE and CURVY FOR HIM!

And for fans of college romances (with a twist, of course . . .) try theCURVY IN COLLEGE Series!

Finally, if you want longer books, try my 23 full-length novels in these over-the-top series: CURVES FOR SHEIKHS and CURVES FOR SHIFTERS!

Love,
Anna.

∞

Books by Annabelle Winters

The CURVES FOR SHEIKHS Series
Curves for the Sheikh
Flames for the Sheikh
Hostage for the Sheikh
Single for the Sheikh
Stockings for the Sheikh
Untouched for the Sheikh
Surrogate for the Sheikh
Stars for the Sheikh
Shelter for the Sheikh
Shared for the Sheikh
Assassin for the Sheikh
Privilege for the Sheikh
Ransomed for the Sheikh
Uncorked for the Sheikh
Haunted for the Sheikh
Grateful for the Sheikh
Mistletoe for the Sheikh
Fake for the Sheikh

The CURVES FOR SHIFTERS Series
Curves for the Dragon
Born for the Bear
Witch for the Wolf
Tamed for the Lion
Taken for the Tiger

The CURVY FOR HIM Series
The Teacher and the Trainer
The Librarian and the Cop
The Lawyer and the Cowboy
The Princess and the Pirate

The CEO and the Soldier
The Astronaut and the Alien
The Botanist and the Biker
The Psychic and the Senator

THE CURVY FOR THE HOLIDAYS SERIES
Taken on Thanksgiving
Captive for Christmas
Night Before New Year's
Vampire's Curvy Valentine
Flagged on the Fourth
Home for Halloween

THE CURVY FOR KEEPS SERIES
Summoned by the CEO
Given to the Groom

THE DRAGON'S CURVY MATE SERIES
Dragon's Curvy Assistant
Dragon's Curvy Banker
Dragon's Curvy Counselor
Dragon's Curvy Doctor
Dragon's Curvy Engineer
Dragon's Curvy Firefighter
Dragon's Curvy Gambler

THE CURVY IN COLLEGE SERIES
The Jock and the Genius
The Rockstar and the Recluse
The Dropout and the Debutante
The Player and the Princess
The Fratboy and the Feminist

WWW.ANNABELLEWINTERS.

Printed in Great Britain
by Amazon